**Praise for**

# Swallow it Down

"A love story as passionate and intelligent as it is beautiful." *–Alta Hensley, USA TODAY bestselling author*

"Make room on your bookshelf. Sultry, gentle, and corrupt, this is a romance that satisfies!" *–Myra Danvers, USA TODAY bestselling author*

"Sumptuous and grand! Addison Cain is at her best!" *–Zoe Blake, USA TODAY bestselling author*

# Swallow it Down

By

Addison Cain

ISBN: 978-1-950711-59-8

Cover art by Raven Designs

# Chapter One

Dripping, swampy sweat had gathered between Eugenia's breasts. Her mouth a desert. Knowing exactly how foul the act was, she delved dirty fingers between slimy mounds to bring the salty brine to parched lips.

And she sucked them clean, ignoring the taste of road dust.

Scrambling to cover exposed skin, cleavage was concealed. From head to toes, her body fully draped to protect from the relentless sun. That same protection half the reason she was melting alive in no man's land.

Sweat. Or burn and sweat. A lose-lose situation.

Wide-brimmed hat, woven by hand and ugly as the day was long, kept the sun off her face. A bandana kept the dust out of her mouth. Layers of repurposed tee-shirts, badly sewn together animal skins, jeans, sneakers on the verge of losing their soles. Torn bits and bobs, a sea of safety pins and animal gut thread keeping her just as fashionably disgusting as everyone else since the world ended.

And the goddamn sun was relentless, miles yet until she might reach where Fresh Water marked her map.

It had been two days.

Two days without fluids was enough to kill in this kind of heat.

A lapping lakeshore—spanned by the raggedy stone bridge underfoot—was just another reminder that nothing could be trusted. Murky, undrinkable water taunted travelers. Water that had tempted many to take a sip. Eugenia had seen enough corpses on the road not to fall for nature's trick.

Not to listen to the sweet splashes as she pined for a drink.

It had once been so easy to grab a bottle of chilled water from the fridge. To not question the source or the safety. Food had been abundant and full of variety. People used words like *organic, vegan, prime...*

Now? Not so much. Eat what you find or don't eat at all. And that included the rare expired snack food that one would think might be exciting when the menu often included grubs, but really... the taste of *before* didn't come with a sense of nostalgia. It came with a knife of remembrance.

The stone bridge. The water. The dead forest taunted her enough with what the world had been. A rare find of Cheetos just pissed her off.

Humid air rustled through branches, but there was no whisper of leaves sighing as trees swayed. Only the bony noise of clicking, snapping wood.

Pathetic last words, but worth muttering. "What I wouldn't give for air conditioning."

The man plodding on at her side grumbled, "They got that up in city. If you'd just go to one, you can pay for cool air like everyone else."

John wasn't the worst companion she'd met on the road. Of a similar age, strong enough to carry his own pack and contribute, he was the quiet sort. Only got handsy with her once. Learned his lesson and remembered the manners his mother must have taught him before nuclear war fucked up everything everywhere.

"Need I remind you, John, this *shortcut* was your idea." He'd strongly suggested this very route, leaning over her without so much as brushing her shoulder when they came to a crossroads and she had to decide left or right.

With a slanted grin, he shrugged. "According to your map, this trail took two days off the journey to Fresh Water."

It wasn't a trail if the road was paved, but there was really no point in correcting him. Especially since she had agreed. The reason she'd agreed? Because it also kept them farther from the marked settlements on her map.

Even better, travelers avoided the dead woods under the false assumption that the forest was toxic. But there were no char marks or wilting. None of the telltale signs that hinted at radiation. The trees were dead, true, but they were also decaying. Irradiated woods didn't decay, because they lacked the microbes responsible for recycling organic matter. These trees died after the bombs fell.

Gypsy Moths.

The forest died when, year after year, caterpillars decimated their leaves—damaging the tree's ability to respirate and gather energy from the sun. Trunks fell and rotted like they were supposed to. Many lay in the road, slowly turning to sawdust.

There were bugs to eat. There were animals to hunt. There were other things growing like weeds on a grave, which meant there was also rain.

Not that Eugenia had enjoyed a sudden thunderstorm or the relief of water she might actually drink falling from the sky. From the look of the dried-out body face down in the middle of the bridge, that poor soul hadn't felt the rain either.

Rushing to pillage the corpse's pack, John pulled the zipper and found… nothing of value.

Eugenia could have told him that. If the person had water, they wouldn't have died on the middle of a bridge, face down and mostly ignored by the wildlife.

Let the man moan and curse.

John's frustration was hers; it was everyone's in the dead world where nothing was easy and everything hurt.

A world greedy humans ruined.

A spoiled world in which Eugenia had been crushing her second year of med school. Harvard, full scholarship.

Then the bombs fell; cities were wiped away in a blink. She'd been camping with friends. Friends who were all dead now, or being whored. Or died being whored. She didn't know.

Couldn't think about it too hard. Just like she wouldn't think about who the corpse might have been.

Because whatever existed before was gone.

The dark ages were back with a vengeance, and *City*. City was a cesspool. Didn't matter which one. No sanitation, roving gangs always fighting for territory, the only way most women might make a buck was on their backs.

And considering the extreme increase in violence against women once the world went to hell, there weren't all that many women left.

So fuck City. And considering the types she'd kept up with since the fall, fuck men in general.

John wasn't so bad. But if he looked at her with that puppy stare one more time, she just might pop him in the mouth.

Leaning against a crumbling stone side rail, she watched John pick through the corpse's pockets, wondering when someone would be doing that to her. And boy would they be disappointed. She had nothing others would find valuable in her pack—the pack itself faded from the blue it had been when new. Torn here and there. Empty of supplies. Heavy, because no matter how bad things got, both volumes of *Nelson's Textbook of Pediatrics* went where she went.

He flipped the corpse over to rifle through what rotting tatters might conceal, the body seeming to smile up at her.

Eugenia didn't smile back.

"We need to get moving." Or this was how she was going to die.

On an endless stone bridge in dangerous, unknown territory, seeking water that was so close she could taste it. Going mad from the sound of tainted drink just a few feet away.

No different than the other bodies they'd found on the road. The whole bodies, the bloated bodies, the dried bodies, and… well... the bits of bodies left after wild dogs found supper.

Man's best friend wasn't so friendly once it started starving.

Which was a pity. Eugenia had grown up with such a great mutt. She still liked dogs. And they liked her too… for a snack.

Killing that first pup in self-defense had been harder than knifing a man trying to get into her pants.

And they all tried.

Which was precisely why she'd been forced to leave her former accommodation, again, and make her way south to new territory.

Where she'd picked up John wallowing on the side of the road. Where she didn't make small talk but shared her supplies.

Everyone held on to something from the past.

John's seemed to be a sense of optimistic stupidity.

Eugenia's was sheer stubbornness and an undying sense of anger that—thanks to a shit president and a fucked-up world—all her dreams had been blown to ash. All her hard work, all the sacrifices she had made to achieve her goals… useless.

Two years of med school did not make one a doctor. A medic, in theory. Which had been handy when there was nothing to trade. But a medic with tits wasn't safe.

She learned that lesson in the first disease-riddled settlement. AKA, the shanty town of Wellspring.

Pretty name for an awful place.

And in the years since, there wasn't any place she wandered by that wasn't awful. Might as well pick one and plant her flag. Give up on her life as a vagrant. Live where sewage collected on the streets and everyone was sick from dirty water and improper hygiene. Try to make things better.

But, if they didn't get moving, she was going to die on that long, stone bridge, never knowing air conditioning again. John would probably take her stuff and die a mile or two up the path. Another traveler would loot his corpse. Just as she had looted bodies for years and pretended not to cry.

There wasn't any moisture for tears now. No point in regrets. But still, that kernel of anger festered, because her perfect future had been stolen by power-mongering boneheads. And six years of living a hard life had not broken her as quickly as it had the others.

Which was unfair.

Why care anymore? Why keep looking for a good place and good people?

“Do you see that?” John, wasting precious energy, waved his arm toward a portion of the lake obscured by dead trees.

“Yup, it’s water.”

“I didn’t think the stories were real, but I’ll be damned. They even got power!”

Electricity was only in City, and even there it was hard to come by, spotty, and cost more than just a cock in the cunt. Anal. That’s what it cost.

Yet, a glitter broke through the copse of decaying trees. Electric light. Which meant water.

Which meant survival.

Already making a mental list of the crap in her pack, trying to scrounge up any idea of what to trade for a full canteen. Shamefully daydreaming of air conditioning and a soft bed.

Knowing full well that an ocean liner had no business in a freshwater lake. That electricity didn't exist in the no man's land on her map. And that she'd gone too long without hydration and was hallucinating.

"Wait." The word was dry, so dry that even though she tried to stop him, John had already begun to run toward the shore. Splashing through sludge, having left his valuables right there on the shore, he dove in, swimming toward the enormous, shining boat.

Something wasn't right.

Who uses electricity when the sun is up? That awful gut feeling that kept her as safe as one might be in this new world clenched so hard it stole her breath. This wasn't a good place. This wasn't a good place if no one knew about it and no map she'd seen marked a moored, massive ship large enough to hold thousands.

But there were people on the landing, coming out at John's hollering. There was a red-carpeted gangplank leading up to the upper levels, welcoming passengers as if they were about to take Eugenia's dreamed-of cruise to the Bahamas.

There would be water. Filtration systems that pumped out water she could actually drink.

"John, come back!" But he ignored her, swimming on.

And she could see those few gathered outside were armed. Men pointing right at her as if to say, *"Collect that."*

Because *this was a bad place*.

And thanks to John, they had seen her.

Options were limited. Swim across the lake and face whatever might be found on her terms. Or, wait for the party already boarding a dinghy to come chase her down in the woods.

She didn't have the strength to run. She didn't have the strength to swim.

But no way on God's dead earth was she going to stand on the shore and be collected.

Potentially drowning in that lake would be better than dying under strangers, chased down by the men earnestly slicing oars through water to reach her.

Men who didn't call out a greeting. Men who looked large and well fed.

And don't forget those guns. Big ones.

Considering it was so fucking hot, why not take a final swim?

Let them see she was not afraid. That she never buckled. That she was smarter than leading them on a merry chase through dead woods.

And that was that.

Off went the hat, the backpack with her precious volumes, the outer layers that would come between her filthy skin and cool, murky water. In she went, swimming for the ship. Knowing she'd never make it.

But she did.

The human condition wouldn't let her sink. Delirious, the body fought the mind and she cut through the water like a fish. Fingers reached the bobbing gangplank, having somehow passed the boat, somehow passed John, who splashed in her wake.

A stranger's firm hands pulled her from the lake, where she fell immediately to her back, staring up at a sun so blinding she couldn't make out the shadowed faces standing over her.

"Well, aren't you a pretty one?" Someone was pawing at her face, turning her chin and brushing wet, red curls off her cheek.

Trying to swat off the attention was almost more effort than her exhausted muscles might put forth. "Hands off the goods."

"And bossy to boot."

The sounds of her companion being pulled from the water, of his sputtering and coughing, were ignored. Eugenia, still blinded by the sun but doing her damnedest to point her eyes in the direction of the dark figure hovering closest, muttered, "Mister, just tell me one thing. You got air conditioning on this ship?"

A masculine chuckle was the only answer supplied.

Her companion coughed, then sucked in a breath to say, "Brought the girl for sale. As you can see, she's a beauty. A great ride too."

John. Fucking puppy-eyed John.

*How dare he*! After she'd hunted for him, shared resources... allowed him to travel with her and glimpse the precious map.

Even though someone held a canteen to her lips, even when clean water warmed by the sun splashed her tongue and was gulped. Right then, right when that water hit her gut, she knew it. John had been planning to sell her all along. That's why the pussy kept pushing for City. That's why he suggested the *shortcut* when his whining never won her.

His voice was coming closer. John crawled near where she guzzled. "Do we have a deal for the girl?"

"No." Authoritative, definite.

Maybe there was a God.

Or maybe there was just nothing but evil. "A slave can't sell a slave. You want water, boy. You work for it. If you don't work, you get tossed over with the rest who failed to pull their weight."

In raggedy underclothes, head pounding, muscles noodley, Eugenia found the strength to lean up on an elbow and spit every drop of life-saving water in her mouth at the traitor. "Pig!"

The same man who had deemed her a slave at first glance ordered, "Get her off the ramp before that creamy skin burns. Take her to the women on Level 15—*in the air conditioning*. Have them clean her up and keep her alive. This siren's too valuable to let die."

Fighting with the little strength she had, biting, hoarse screams, and pathetic flopping did nothing to keep her from being shouldered like a knapsack.

It wasn't a short walk, but she didn't give up, powerless to move her arms more than a sorry swing but sharp with her tongue. She threatened the stranger's life, swore she'd tear off his cock if he put it anywhere near her. His mother. His family. Creative in her expletives until a door opened and cool air blasted her back.

There really was air conditioning on that boat! One taste of it on her skin and she went from spitting hellcat to sobbing wreck.

The trivial thing she'd craved most from the life stolen when the bombs fell was just as divine as she remembered.

"Hey, Joan, here's a new one. Captain wants her cleaned up and kept alive. Level 15."

"Well"—a woman spoke, a no-nonsense, middle-aged voice—"won't that just get the men frothing at the mouth? And just look at all that red hair."

"Temper to match. She's a biter." Hefting Eugenia down against something soft and forgotten, the bruiser who dragged her into air-conditioned hell warned Joan, "Watch yourself."

"Yeah, I heard you. Now go. No men are allowed up here until the bell."

# Chapter Two

Water enough to make her belly poke out, blessed air conditioning, a bed with real sheets that were so clean her dirt made a mark... it should have been bliss.

It wasn't.

According to the solitary porthole in her room—a porthole too small to climb through and too high above the lake to survive the fall should she dislocate a shoulder and squeeze out—Eugenia had measured two days.

Time to recover from dehydration, most of it spent sleeping, drinking, eating food that was delivered by the no-nonsense Joan. Using an honest to God toilet when her taxed kidneys continued to do their job.

A porthole with a bird's-eye view of the cliff face that concealed the ship from any wandering travelers brave enough to dare the seemingly endless, decaying wood.

Dogs howled each night, the familiar, dreaded sound sending her to her feet, heart in her throat as she reached for a knife that wasn't there. As she scrambled to hide. Only to find herself blinking in the dark. Confused. Protected by inches of solid steel.

No stray pack was getting at her there. Something worse would try.

Her gut never lied.

And it wasn't like she hadn't been in a similar position before. But always in a ruin, a hut, a pen, a ditch in the ground. Never a massive ocean liner with working electricity and flushing toilets.

New situations required a new perspective. Her body required rest.

She'd die without water.

And water was delivered aplenty, with *ice* clicking against the side of the glass. They had ice machines, for fuck's sake! They had guns, which meant they probably had the ammunition to fire them.

They had resources to feed what had been deemed a slave, and the luxury of time to allow that slave to be more than… what she'd seen so many other women turned into.

Bland food three times a day, mostly stew, brought to her like she was some princess in a tower. Yet no morsel ever served with any sort of utensil—heaven forbid she try to make a weapon out of a freaking spoon. Only a bit of crusty bread that, in itself, was so rare she gobbled it down despite the brick in her stomach.

They had ovens. They had stoves. *They made bread.*

No one, save Joan, entered her room. No men came jeering at the door. There were no squabbles in the halls over who got to fuck her first.

When she yelled for answers or threw her weight against the door, no soul took her bait.

Another stark reminder that this was very different compared to all her other situations of capture in the past.

Two days turned to three before her solitude was broken by more than a tray and congenial older woman. Joan arrived with orders.

First, a shower overseen by Eugenia's overpolite taskmaster. Joan, standing over her, making certain every inch was scrubbed clean of filth, that stray body hair was removed. Joan scrubbing caked mud from red curls when Eugenia's shampooing skills were apparently under par. Joan slathering her locks with conditioner to take out the snarls, pulling a comb through Eugenia's wet mane until it felt like half her hair had been ripped from her skull.

Tsking, shaking her head at another errant tangle, Joan complained, "Young lady… you had three days to wash, and I have to be the one to come in and make you? Do you have any idea how you smelled?"

Well excuse the fuck out of her. "How was I supposed to know that water was safe?"

And why on earth would Eugenia want to wash off her filth and potentially grow appealing to the *things* that crept around this place?

Under her breath, the older woman continued to fight a knot that would probably need to be cut out of her hair. "Can't have washed this mop in years."

It was less that she was naked in front of a stranger, and more that the stranger's snark was really getting on Eugenia's nerves. "Oh yeah, every chance I get, I trot right up to the Four Seasons and book the presidential suite, followed by a day at the spa. How long has it been since you've been out there, lady? Let someone get a glimpse of the goods and you'll end up on a whore ship, shaving your legs and armpits in front of a stranger. Oh, and there will be a man with his back to you, two feet away in case you try to use the safety razor to attack Madame Joan, wrangler of unwilling women who'd would really like off this boat."

That earned a smirk, Joan's silver bob better suited to a business meeting than stranger scrubbing. "But you owe a debt now. Food, water, two nights' board. Oh, and those clothes you so kindly refused to wear. Don't get me wrong; the men would love to see the new girl naked on her first day, but let's take things one step at a time."

"How the hell did you even come by clothes like that out here?" Lacy panties. A plaid, pleated mini skirt. A shirt designed to tie under her breasts and leave her belly exposed. "This is a stripper's version of naughty Catholic schoolgirl outfit… and I'm not a whore."

"No, you're not. They won't be paying you." Joan didn't mince words, which Eugenia had to admit was somewhat appreciated, considering the circumstances. "They won't be paying you for your time. You, young lady, are an indentured guest."

Fancy language was a tool smart people used to confuse stupid ones. Leaving Eugenia with a *don't even try it* smirk as she said, "My mom used to call me 'young lady,' but only when I was in trouble."

"You have been a bit of trouble, but that's nothing a few weeks' hard labor won't wear out of you."

"Or, and hear me out." Raising her hands and not at all concerned that the bodyguard was listening, Eugenia gave her most winning smile. "All the women can mutiny, poison the men, and take over the boat. We could christen this ship *New Amazonia*. Eh? Good idea, right?"

"It takes a crew of three-hundred strong men to keep this ship running, to gather food, to manage maintenance and power, to make repairs, to fight off invaders, and run trade. Sorry, young lady, but I'm comfortable… and you will be too once you accept the world isn't what it was."

"It's not my fault all you older idiots voted for the wrong president! I wasn't even eighteen when that potato stole his first term. *You* killed this world, and now I am expected to whore in it?" There was no question of the bitterness hanging tight in Eugenia's heart. None at all, when she added, "Thanks, but no."

Bitterness it didn't seem practical ol' Joan shared. "From the stories circulating, that John fellow said you whored plenty."

"Yeah, well John is a lying sack of shit."

"You're not the first girl brought here by their beau. Just be glad you're not chained down in the engine room like he is. He'll have to slog at least six months before he's given an option to win tickets. You get all of this." Gesturing around the tiny bathroom and the adjacent cubicle with the twin bed, Joan knew the same thing Eugenia did. This was actually… fine living these days.

A shower, a mattress, the world's sluttiest outfit—and that was not an exaggeration. The world did not make clothes like that anymore. As far as where these men scrounged up lace panties, Eugenia could not even begin to guess. "What are tickets? I thought you said no one got paid."

Tiny scissors snipping through overgrown hair, Joan went from detangling to barbering. "Consider them currency. Men win or trade for tickets that get them up to Level 15, to enjoy the company of ladies."

"Well, I'll be damned. A raffle for pussy. And I will be getting paid. So… back to the statement where I refuse to whore."

"There are rules, missy." Apparently, her sass wasn't as funny as it *had* been. Barking at the guard to move doors, Joan pocketed the safety razor. A razor Eugenia strongly suspected all the women shared.

Which had to be commented upon. "Sharing that razor could lead to a spread of hepatitis just so pits and legs might be smooth for some greased-up dirtbag. It's a tiny virus and only takes one nick. But hey, were all just slaves here."

"Don't want to slave? Earn your ransom. It's the only way any female steps off this boat."

So there were more options than attempting an escape out of the ship's only exit... several floors down, through man-infested halls? "How many tickets? How do I get them?"

"How many is up to the captain. Each girl has a different price. As far as earning those slips of paper, you trade for them." The woman dared shove lacy panties and the slutty Halloween costume right into Eugenia's chest. "You trade the one commodity you got."

Incentive for a slave to think she might actually buy her way out. The psychological mind fuck was… epic. But Eugenia had not planned to specialize in psychiatry. "And let me guess. The price goes up with each offence."

That earned her a snide smirk. "You are as smart as you seem."

"Anyone ever paid it?" Because there was no way the game wasn't horribly rigged.

Pride shown in an honest smile. The pride of a free woman who lived in luxury. "I did."

Jaw hanging, Eugenia shook her head. "But… you're still here."

"By choice. I can walk out that door anytime I wish, take a walk by the lake. Visit City."

Growing angry, feeling her color rise, Eugenia grit it out again. "But you're still here!"

The indomitable Joan *madamed* by choice. For air conditioning and comfort. "The ship is a haven, but we all must do our part."

"Such as try to convince the new girl to shave her public hair."

"I let you keep it. Don't think it will keep them off you. You're a novelty for now. Expect lots of offers. Earn your tickets while you can. Exuberance is always encouraging." And with that final statement, Joan put a hand to the guard's back and shut the door.

The lock clicked, Eugenia standing wrapped in a white towel, holding lacy sin.

***

"Every girl is assigned a table."

"Every *woman*," Eugenia corrected, gnawing her cuticle as she inspected the ship's festive version of the lido deck. A striped awning covered six cushioned booths. Booths which would each seat five men—two ladies assigned to entertain the table with witty banter and smiles. Other ladies serving food. All *women* on rotation each night.

That meant thirty men out of three hundred had the opportunity to be entertained by sixteen women each night. Oh, and there were no nights off. Not unless one began to menstruate, in which case they were given the length of their womb's monthly cleansing to rest.

How gallant the captain's rules were.

Wearing a different though equally inappropriate costume, the woman who'd been assigned Table #2, Brooke, threw Eugenia a look. It was anything but mean. More of an *I get it; believe me, I do* look. "Every night before dinner is served, a game is set up to entertain our guests in the hall. The winner pulls the ball that decides which *women* are selected for the end-of-dinner cleanup."

"Which means?" Because scrubbing the floor didn't sound half bad.

"It means that the girls from that table have to stand still as the men dump all their uneaten food and leftover beer on us while they laugh and we… take it."

"You're joking…" Not only was the concept of uneaten food beyond grasping, but why on God's green earth dump it on poor, captive women?

With a sigh, her tablemate tossed glossy, dark hair over her shoulder. The pin-straight strands swung, as she continued, "As you're new, the game will be rigged. They're going to call #2, and you and I will be tonight's dumpster."

"None of this is making sense to me."

"It will. There's a reason for all of it. I'm two-hundred thousand tickets away from getting out of here, and I'd appreciate it if you didn't cause trouble and up my price." Pretty, Korean-American, petite, and perfect, Brooke plumped her breasts and adjusted her skirt.

"Jesus."

"You nailed it." Brown eyes far too old in a face so young held hers. "We didn't pick this world, but we're stuck in it. But us girls should stick together."

Eugenia opened her mouth, only for the petite beauty to interject. "If you correct me one more time, newbie, you'll lose the only ally you have tonight. Girl? Woman? It doesn't matter. All that matters to me is getting off this boat."

"I'm sorry." And she truly was. It seemed no one was here by choice, save Joan. And Brooke had already worked this life for over a year. "I won't cause you trouble."

"Thank you." Brown eyes darting side to side, Brooke leaned closer to whisper, "Which is why I'm going to warn you there will be glass shards in your food. Don't eat it."

"What?" Swallowing shards of glass might puncture the stomach and require immediate surgery that did not exist in the shithole new world! "You're joking, right?"

"Not all the girls are happy you're here. More competition for tickets, favors, comforts… you know?"

And though she'd had three days to think it over, to recall how close she had been to the reaper on that stone bridge, Eugenia felt reality sink deeper than any witty tenacity. "I'm going to die on this boat."

"Probably. So make the best of things. Lift up your skirt and just take it, as many as you can before they are bored of you." And with that final proclamation, the doors opened, and the *guests* arrived.

Boisterous and loud, they poured in. The cleanest group of men Eugenia had seen since the bombs fell. Hair combed, shirts pressed. Scrubbed, smiling, and aware of the system, they found their seats with little trouble—their prize for saving and hard work achieved.

And though not every last one of them was staring right at Eugenia, the majority were.

At red curls that fell without frizzy tangles. At skin too fair to withstand sun. At defiance.

She met their intrigue with a sinister curl to her lip. Because fuck tickets.

That game was for the desperate. Which of course she was. But she was also smart. Top of her class. Knew where every last artery pulsed and the exact amount of time it would take a man to bleed out from a *minor* puncture wound.

And it burned to know that she would have made an amazing pediatric surgeon yet never would achieve that attainable goal. Not in this world where women shared a razor and the lord only knew how many STDs were spread each night at these parties.

A bony elbow nudged her ribs. "Smile, goddammit."

No. There was nothing here to smile about. But Eugenia did it out of solidarity.

The smile of a stray warning off a pack of hungry wolves.

# Chapter Three

Rules, rules, and more rules. Turns out there was more to the captain's *way of things* than just winning the chance to be serviced by the ladies. There was rank in the order the men arrived. In seat placement. In the absolute absurdity of the baking sheets two men waved to signal they were the hosts to their hostesses.

Booths that sat five large men—men grown strong on regular feedings and hard labor—had no room for the women. So, where did the ladies go? On the cookie sheet, on the men's laps. Preventing the inevitable erection from gaining purchase where it was not yet welcome.

Because rules.

"I'm supposed to sit on that?" It was all too silly to grasp. She wasn't a pastry.

"Yes. You're very pretty. My name is Neil." Broad of shoulder and tall enough to be intimidating, a man in his early thirties patted the cookie sheet with a kind smile. “Come on now. I won’t bite.”

“To be clear”—because burly men were approaching and a scene would not help her cause, Eugenia bit down on her pride and hopped on that lap—“I’m not having sex with any of you.”

Neil seemed so gentile as he put a hand to her bare belly and spread his fingers. “It’s your first night. And you’re lucky you got placed with such an upstanding group of men. We don’t bend the rules. Unless you give us permission or take reward, your company is pleasure enough.”

Pulling her to rest against his chest, finding resistance, the hand on her stomach didn’t move up toward a breast or down to tuck into that insanely short skirt. Planted, it did nothing but be. Despite her tension, her wide eyes, her desire to elbow him right in his nose.

“No need to brace. We can touch what clothing doesn’t cover. I just want to hold a girl against me for a few hours.”

Which sounded so reasonable, like such a trick, that Eugenia wasn't falling for it.

Cleaned-up Cookie Sheet Guy wasn't bad-looking. The opposite, in fact. Fair-haired, sun-darkened skin, polished, no rancid reek of sweat. He was even funny as he conversed with his comrades. One of whom had Brooke in a very different embrace. A familiar cuddle, a cuddle requiring he place tickets on the table to expose her breasts and palm her lace-clad rump.

Fucking carnival tickets. The red ones that came on a roll.

Women had all been reduced to a sideshow game prize.

Dinner was served. The men dined on mouthwatering grilled meat so fragrant Eugenia salivated. Steak? How in the hell did they have steak? Raising cattle required land, feed, a skill in animal husbandry. It required lots of water...

Her clay bowl of slop was nothing in comparison. And Brooke's warning was, in fact, true.

There were shards of glass buried in chunks of God only knew what.

Managing to eat with one hand, as if moving his digits from her belly might make her run out of reach, Neil held up a fork of perfectly cooked, dripping ribeye. "Would you like to share?"

Unsmiling, she kept her gaze forward. "No, thank you."

"It's just one bite. It won't cost you much."

Yeah, she was going to die on this ship. Probably from starvation and stubbornness.

"Treat me like a whore again and I'll break your nose, *Neil*." At that, she turned to meet his kinda-pretty blue eyes. "I might not know all the rules, but I know full well that when a boy says 'it won't cost you much,' he's full of shit."

"Man," Neil corrected, taking that perfect bite with a smile. Chewing with his mouth closed, clearly happy to enjoy the robust flavors, he swallowed before adding, "Half my steak for one kiss on the mouth."

Boy did these idiots underestimate just how expensive survival off this ship had been. “I don’t know where you’ve been. And as tempting as your pretty steak is, I’d rather save my skin from herpes, syphilis, chlamydia, gonorrhea. This pit must be a cesspool of disease, all the cross contamination, the—”

“Stop right there, little lady. Fresh as you are, *we’re* taking a risk on you. Not the other way around. All men are required to wait six months before they can even petition to join this soiree. Secondly, each man, each night he earns the right to dine, goes through a pretty uncomfortable medical check.”

“With petri dishes and blood work? This ship doesn’t have a lab, a microbiologist, or a hood.” Why had the world grown so dumb? “Many STDs are invisible upon visual inspection, especially concerning men. So, pleasant southern accent and all, Neil, I do not want to trade a bite of food for my physical or mental wellbeing.”

"I like this one!" another man at the table—one who clearly had not earned a cookie sheet or a girl on his lap—said with a grin.

And what was there to say to that? Nothing.

Hearty, healthy men wanted to fuck. Lived in a society that set up the opportunity to earn tickets though labor or trade. Had women sit on their laps with only cookie sheets, scraps of clothing, and the barter of tickets or favors between them.

And, if Brooke had spoken the truth, these same *charming* men would dump their home-brew beer and leftover food over women's heads while they walked out the door. As if they had not just fucked them or shared hours of cuddles.

It had been three days since Eugenia almost died from dehydration. She was weak and already tired just from bathing and sitting on the lap of the stranger palming her stomach.

But she was far from giving up.

Coquettish, batting her lashes, she said, "I'll tell you what, sweetheart. Take a big bite of my soup, and I'll show you the best ride of your life."

"Don't!" Brooke shouted, reaching forward to knock the bowl over before Neil might grab the spoon.

And there they were, shards of glass, of clay, bits of jagged rock. Did these women not think she'd chew?

Probably not. Everyone must have been dumped on the ship starving.

"What happened here?" Joan, like the final judgement herself, landed at the table.

"I spilled my soup when I saw broken glass on the spoon. Brooke was kind enough to try to stop the mess." A mess that was spilling into the laps of the scrambling guests Eugenia had been ordered to entertain. "Chain me and whip me, Madame. I'm too weak from hunger to satisfy these men. And though glass contains silica, it's nutrient deficient in all other ways."

"For Christ's sake, child. Your flair for drama is—"

"What is it? Worse than hidden shards of glass in your food? What good is a slave of breeding age if she's a corpse? Three days max, these men could hump the body before it began to swell. After that, it will release gas and fluids. Ever seen a corpse fart? I have. It's extremely unsexy."

It was clear Joan didn't want to laugh, that she fought back the tic at the corner of her mouth to snap her fingers at the women tasked with serving the ship's fancy soiree. "Clean up the mess. Fresh tablecloth, extra beer for these men, a half-cup for Brooke. Eugenia has chosen to fast tonight."

As pretty, half-naked women rushed forward, Eugenia set her elbow to the soiled tablecloth, pinning it in place when they thought to tug the mess away. So they had to look at her when she said, "Indeed, I have. Call it a hunger strike in female solidarity. After all, we only won the right to vote about one-hundred years ago. But then the world blew up… and now here we all are. I think we should petition for an increase in minimum wage. Fifteen tickets an hour."

Plump-lipped with waving chestnut locks, one of the women wiping up the mess hissed, "Shut up before he hears you!"

Oh, let whoever *he* was hear. But not until the other women heard her first. Voice dropping to a whisper, unsure if the striking brunette was even the culprit, Eugenia said, "Serve me glass again and I'll use it to cut your carotid artery while you're sleeping."

Eugenia's elbows went up, and just like that, the table was clean. Fresh linen in place, beer aplenty for the men, and nothing but a baking sheet between the majority of Neil's lap and Eugenia's ass.

How had society come to this? How did that collection of adults seem so comfortable with the rules?

Looking to Neil, Eugenia asked, "We all can agree that this is ridiculous, right?"

"You don't have to go hungry." Despite those spread fingers on her belly, Neil had been remarkably polite… aside from the offers of a kiss for a bite of cow. "Just eat what's left." And it visibly pained him greatly to add, "I'll give it to you."

Never look a gift cow in the mouth. Especially when the majority of a steak was on offer. As she had agreed not to touch anything sharper than a spoon, lest she receive a beating that had been described in enviable detail, Eugenia scooped up the steak and ate it just as she'd eat roasted squirrel. All hands and teeth and hollow-stomach starvation.

They had salt on the ship. They had pepper.

She moaned from the taste.

The cooks made food that took a girl back to before the bombs, before everyone she knew scattered to the wind. Before the universe utterly failed her.

"Well, Neil, if I didn't hate that you were trying to buy me instead of genuinely get to know me, I would give you that kiss. But hey, love is dead. I was sold by an idiot I found wandering the road with no pack. That's mercy. And him being chained in the engine room—or so I have been told—is karma." Picking her teeth with her pinky nail, she cooed, "Tell me, did you sell one of these ladies to have access to steak?"

White teeth in a splendid grin, Neil gave her the dopey puppy look that always ended badly. "I think I could just love you."

"Handsome as you are, the feeling is not mutual."

"You'll change your tune. After all"—southern drawl in full effect—"fate won me your time tonight. You feel like cream, and you smell like strawberries."

"It's the shampoo."

Looking even more enamored than jackass John, Neil rubbed little circles on her belly. The same belly now full of *his* steak. "I'll save up to see you again. Once you settle in, you'll think better of me."

"All just slaves to the machine, eh? Let's fuck until the world totally dies and humans are replaced by radioactive cockroaches. That's the same drivel John tried to feed me too." Throwing an arm over Neil's shoulders, Eugenia set her lips to his ear, whispering, "And guess what? He couldn't get me to fuck him either."

He held a bit tighter. "You're missing the point of the game if you think what the men up here want is sex."

A nasty scoff was offered in response.

"We're lonely, not enough women around no matter how hard we look. If we don't share, we can't function as a unit. You think we don't fall for you? That we don't sacrifice to find baubles and buy favor?"

"You make it sound like I have the power." And, boy, that diatribe was not going to work on her.

But the man's unguarded glance was nothing but exposed. "You do. You even get to keep the babies we're never allowed to hold."

All that steak was about to come up. "Stop talking to me."

“Fine.” But Neil’s response was resigned. Weighted down by God only knew what.

Yet that hand remained on her belly, his chest to her back.

And though that should have eaten up all her attention, in the hour that followed the men’s hard-won dinner, her scrutiny landed on another.

The intruder so close she couldn’t imagine how he had been missed.

Sitting on the floor, jean-clad legs stretched out, and the wall at his back. Not ten feet away. Boots pointed right at her. A man who looked every bit the cowboy yet utterly a pirate, lounged. So relaxed he had melted into the scenery.

Not dressed as finely as the men who’d spent their tickets for a few hours of shared female company. Lacking the tilted hat over his brow or the bit of hay that should have hung from his lips, he watched all around him in the lazy way of someone not to be trusted.

Eyes of an indecipherable color from this distance took in everything.

And everyone made way for him, unless, like Joan, they approached in reverence.

How odd it was to listen to the madame list a quantity of items required for the *girls*. How easily the captain nodded that he heard her and acquiesced.

He could not have shaved in a week.

Probably smelled more like a man than the perfumed collection at Table #2.

Those boots caught the sun. Polished. Worn yet cared for.

Which spoke about character and habit. Drew Eugenia to slink off the lap of the man who'd traded tickets for a cookie sheet and access to uncovered skin. Yet, it wasn't facing off against the captain that kept her feet going; it was inspecting those boots.

Crouched down until at eye-level, tapping her finger against metal embellishments, she said, "These might just be the cleanest shoes I've seen in six years."

"Your ass is in the air. Unless you're offering to the panting crowd, you might want to tuck your tail."

That voice. Eugenia knew that voice. "It was you who pulled me from the water."

"That I did."

Dragging her gaze from those boots, she ignored all the rest of him—the open shirt, the exposed chest, the dark hair shining and in need of a cut—to get directly to the point. His eyes.

Hazel. Lined. Not a day under forty.

"I want off this ship."

The man might have set a cigarette to his lips and lit it. But there was no cigarette, and lighters were worth more than a fast fuck. "No."

"I won't whore for you." Not ever.

He gave her nothing. "We'll see."

"Listen to me, slaver." She crept nearer, overcoming his legs so they might negotiate eye-to-eye. Woman-to-man. "You'll be disappointed."

The corner of his lips lifted. “I doubt it.”

Had he just winked at her?

Asshole.

Confrontation was no different than an elite university’s oral exam. He was no different than any of the men who might have had her in their clutches for a short time. No different than dirt. A prick deserving of the clinical Eugenia who aced every test and never said die. “This is a ship with three-hundred or so men and less than two dozen women. Where, from what I understand, thirty men a night dump their saliva-laden food and drink on two of the aforementioned women. I’m amazed there hasn’t been some outbreak that killed off half your *slaves*. And, as condoms are no longer produced and those available would have expired last April, I’d rather not be exposed to gonorrhea, which asymptomatic men spread despite the supposed physical examination all these rapist undergo—”

It was so fast his backhand landed on her cheek before she’d seen him go from lazy, lounging cowboy to typical violent male. The taste of blood in her mouth, the throb and heat that came each time a man had put his hands on her, led Eugenia to turn her head right back toward the captain. Again, they were eye-to-eye.

Life, tickets, baking sheets, and shared scraps for sex. It wasn't worth it. He needed to know she knew that.

She needed to know how far he'd go.

Limits set parameters for escape. Violence defined a man.

Push hard. Mouth off. Let them know she might be scared, but what did it matter? The whole fucking world was scary.

And this ship, this society he'd designed? No.

Make the big, bad pirate slaver do what the men at her table wouldn't do in the name of rules and trades. Make it public and grotesque in this fake civility. Make a statement. "Captain, if you're going to hit me, put some effort into it. That was barely a swat."

And he obliged, so predictable she hardly blinked an eye when her back hit the deck.

Grip on her throat, his free hand snaking up that sorry excuse for a skirt, he hissed, "You think you've got something more precious—"

But his own efforts, *his own violence*, stopped him dead in his tracks.

She'd known rape might take place before the final stomping, but she had not imagined the asshole would push aside her panties and delve in.

It never went down that way. Ringleaders didn't just force the goods when a profit could be made; they lathered up the crowd. Made a display to get their followers panting in submission.

Yet the captain had, in less than a heartbeat, shove three of his fingers as deep as they might go.

The behavior didn't match the boots.

Rough grip cutting off proper blood supply to her brain, Eugenia still grimaced, squeezing her eyes shut from the burn.

There would be blood on his hand. And by the scandalized look on his face, he had felt the membrane ringing her vaginal opening give under careless penetration. What she had spent a lifetime guarding, he could have traded for a whole herd of cattle. Gone, because she'd goaded him.

And, yes, she grasped that there was no proof of virginity, that all bodies were different, but after enough pap smears, Eugenia knew hers was a bit *more*. That band of skin unstretched and *there*.

Shocked enough to loosen his grip, Eugenia found the air to snarl right in the captain's face, "Get your fingers out of my vaginal canal."

Those fingers fluttered in place of retracting. "It isn't possible…"

Still in her, the sting only growing when he continued to wiggle them as if to make sure it was blood squelching over his touch, Eugenia fought to keep her legs as they were. To show no fear and to remember that she could cry over this later where no one might see. But not now. "Perhaps you find the concept outdated. But believe it or not, I was waiting for a worthy man to spend my life with. What you just stole was my gift to give, not yours to take. You also just made me far less valuable to trade off this ship. Well done."

It was only then she realized how intimate this violence appeared to the crowd. How he hovered over her, inside her still… smiling even as they gathered to watch. "You're a virgin."

The label was a bit sticky, though she had been waiting until marriage to enjoy penetration. "Was. You just tore my hymen, which I will never forgive you for."

"No cock was in you. You're still a virgin."

Heart racing, unwilling to back down, she spat, "Don't debate physiology with me, slaver. Finish what you started. Show me why you polish those boots every day. Show them all just what you really are. A monster who exploits women and sexually assaults strangers."

His hand left her neck, stroking a stray curl off her sweaty forehead. “Oh, they know *exactly* what I am. Just as we all know why I won’t damage a valuable, beautiful, red-haired virgin. The men wouldn’t stand for it.”

“This joke of civility you stage here each night? Utter bullshit.” Rolling her body under his weight as if she stood a chance to displace him, Eugenia added, “I. Will. Not. Whore. For. Fucking. Tickets.”

Fingers still burrowed, her blood making its slow way down her crack, he put his lips to her hair. Breathed her in. “Give head for tickets if you don’t want to be fucked. You can save your pussy for your nonexistent Prince Charming.”

“What an elegant solution!” Though he was still in her and it still hurt, she made sure the whole deck heard her crystal-clear. “Try putting a dick near my mouth and I’ll bite it off. Let me off this boat now and save yourself a pile of trouble. I’ll upset your system. I’ll twist your rules. I’ll take the beatings.

Hear me when I say this. I've faced down far worse than any of you."

"Well then, siren." Finally, the captain pulled his fingers out of her body, pinioning weight against his prize while he inspected the blood on those digits for himself. Red, fresh, and more copious than she'd expected, his three fingers shined crimson in the setting sun.

And she stung where the membrane had been torn, hating to think of what dirt might have been under his nails when he thought to subdue her with something so…

When he took something so…

She wouldn't call it precious. Because it wasn't anymore.

Because this world's elders fucked it up for everyone. Long gone were wedding nights and tender men. They had Johns, who she'd saved and who'd tried to trade her person for fucking water.

"The shock will wear off. Look at me."

“What?” That’s right. She was on a ship, dressed like a tramp so she might earn tickets to freedom for sexual favors.

And the man who had just jammed his fingers with true violence inside her was adjusting the gusset of her lacy panties, smearing her thigh with virgin blood.

“Get off of me.” Her voice shook, and she hated herself for it.

“I think you need a drink. Also, just so we’re clear, you’ve added one-hundred thousand tickets to your price.”

Oh, she was going to kill him. Which didn’t need to be said. It was right there in her glare. “I will find a way to take something from you of equal value. Then I will burn your goddamn ship to the bottom of this rancid lake.”

Why was he smiling? “I believe you.”

“You’re smarter than you look.”

After snapping his fingers, Joan appeared out of thin air to his call. How she already had a cup of beer, Eugenia couldn't say. But it was there, and he took it, pressing it to her hands.

"I'm not drinking that shit." A clear head was needed at all times these days.

"Drink it or I'll put my fingers back in and keep them there all night." And he'd enjoy it—his smirk said that plain as day.

But she was no simple opponent. "Do yourself a favor and escort me off the boat."

"Try again, siren." He pushed the earthenware cup closer to her lips, fingers coated in her drying blood.

She would not take a drop into her mouth, considering what might lurk in homebrew garbage… until her eyes cut to Table #2 and the terror on Brooke's face registered.

All of it sunk in at that moment. It was more than this fucked society, air conditioning, whoring, and fingers ripping membranes. It was more than her at stake, which is what made the captain's system so indescribably wrong. Every soul on this ship was tied to a well-oiled machine of expectation and consequence. Eugenia's hostility would cost another far more than it would cost her.

The captain was indeed smarter than the lazy cowboy persona he projected.

And he knew it. And he knew the precise moment she knew it too.

"I will drink. I will go back to my table and *verbally* entertain your men… on one condition."

Voice husky, he said, "I do enjoy negotiation."

"I'll bear Brooke's half of the responsibility when you command your men to dump their food and drink on our bodies as if we are worthless come dumpsters. And I take on the remainder of her tickets."

"You'd rather play the hero than the damsel?" Cocky, already lazing back without going to the trouble of wiping his fingers on his shirt, the captain said, "You're not going to like it."

"Isn't that the point?"

Hazel eyes closing as if to drowse, he muttered, "Very smart. Drink up."

She did. Her first real taste of beer since the bombs. Good beer to boot.

Brooke got to go inside, lighter twenty-thousand tickets—not close to half of what she still owed, but enough to make her glow with appreciation.

It took more willpower than Eugenia anticipated to get up off the deck and resume her *duties* at Table #2 alone. The virgin jokes, the way the men—and not just from her table—all of them, seemed to find a reason to drop by, staring at the smeared blood on her exposed thigh.

They touched it.

Because those were the rules. Anything not covered by clothing was fair game.

So she described, in detail, how each sexually transmitted disease affected the body and mind. Puss, sores, sterility. All of it. The internet had been gone for six years, but in its place, human imagination had become vivid again. Enough, but not all of them, were scared away by graphic detail, so she didn't start screaming.

No one raped her. Sex was taking place, *for tickets*, at the other tables. Where other young women dressed like pre-war strippers bent over with no foreplay and took it.

And then, after hours of conversation and fake smiles, every last bastard at the party walked past, dumping his food and beer on Eugenia's head on their way out the door. Laughing at the uptight virgin with the big tits and puffy nipples you could see through her shirt if you splashed leftover beer just right.

As Brooke had warned her, every rule existed for a reason. And it didn't take a would-be pediatric surgeon to figure it out. No woman would grow attached to a man who did this to her. No man would see her as a person in need of help. The nightly event was a show and nothing more. With no winners, and one massive loser.

Her.

She did cry that night in the shower, alone where no one could see.

# Chapter Four

The routine was much easier to fall into than Eugenia would ever admit to herself. Wake up, alone, her room the perfect temperature, thanks to air conditioning.

And get to work.

Swab the deck, swab the toilets, swab her room, swab herself.

It grew painfully clear that Eugenia had no interest in tickets—three weeks having passed without her accepting a single one. Nor another morsel of food, a shiny bauble, nothing. She would sit on the designated lap, the opportunity to host her on a cookie sheet a privilege men paid extra tickets for in those first few days, until they saw the shrew who out-conversed them, outplayed them, and would never fuck them. Her novelty wore off and the other women warmed up.

She wasn't a threat to their freedom or their favorites—though that was also on the list of rules. No favorites allowed. Though even Eugenia had them. Neil wasn't so bad, and he really did just want to hold a woman when he got assigned to her table. But he absolutely fucked at the other tables, waiting in line with the other men, *if* the lady was willing to give him a ride.

Some of the men chose her because sex was not on offer. They wanted real snark, honest conversation, a female mind to connect with. And as she saw it, she hurt for them as much as they sickened her. For all of them. Everyone trapped on the boat, in a dead world, was living out a painful fantasy with no end in sight.

At first, she preferred the nights serving as waitress to the nights serving as hostess to lonely, horny men. But if she was not engaged, she was shadowed.

The captain had struck her that first day. There was no question he'd sexually assaulted her with no thought for her as a person. And now he lurked wherever she went.

After all, her threat to burn down his ship had not been made in vain.

If she was scrubbing dishes in the kitchens, her hair tied up, out of nowhere, a finger would trip down her nape. The first time, she screamed bloody murder, so lost in her thoughts she hadn't heard him coming. And dropped a dish, which shattered over the floor she just mopped.

All southern drawl, he smirked to see her so undone. "You should be more careful with my things. That's another five-thousand tickets."

Hand to her breasts, positive her heartrate was in the unsafe levels, she snarled, "Fuck your tickets, and fuck you too!"

"Anything else you'd like to add?"

"Yes, in fact. I was offered five-thousand tickets last night—the going rate, if I understand correctly—if only I'd bend over the table and take it from some guy named Amos." Crossing her arms under her breasts, she faced him, wet and sweaty, soap bubbles up her arms. "I'd like to think sex is worth more than a single plate. Not that I give a fuck about your ticket scale, but wouldn't you consider your pricing a bit askew?"

"It was a very pretty plate."

"*You* are an asshole." One who liked to get her worked up each time he caught her alone. "Go away. I have chores. Also, I'm menstruating. According to your rules, I don't have to be in the presence of men. Bye now."

Rubbing his hand over the scruff on his cheek, the man's eyes went down to her apron-covered belly. "Are you regular?"

"Keeping a calendar?" It could be exceptionally smart if he was. After all, when making the duties schedule, ovulation wouldn't be the best time for his slaves to service the patrons. Pregnant whores were not as useful.

Reaching past her to grab an apple off the counter, it was like he could read her thoughts.

In her personal space. Much, much too close, a full head taller, he crunched that first bite of forbidden fruit and gave her a wink.

How the hell he even had apples was… something she didn't want to know. How they had any of this bounty couldn't be anything but bad.

"Are you really going to just stand there?" Inches away, so close she could smell him, all woodsy and leather. That she'd nudge him if she turned around and went back to scrubbing dishes.

He took a second bite of apple. Chewed and stared.

She gave it right back to him.

He ate that whole fruit down to the core, smiling as he snacked.

When she just couldn't tolerate another moment of his antics, she groaned to the heavens and threw up her hands. "Fine, stay. I'll leave. After all, it is your ship. I'm just an *endentured guest* here…

trying to wash your *pretty* dishes, so your ugly men have something eat off of when they cash in their tickets to visit your sex slaves on Level 15."

She hadn't made it a step before he ended her retreat, grabbing her by the bicep and yanking her close. "The books in your pack. You a doctor?"

He knew just where to land a verbal blow. Her eye twitched when she stared toward the door and put her weight against his grip. "Do I look old enough to be a doctor?"

"No."

Mimicking his drawl, she tugged against his hold. "Well, aren't you smart?"

"Eugenia." The way he said her name, it was as if he knew all her secrets. "You wrote your name on the inside cover of both books. They were wrapped in plastic to protect them from the elements. Weighed a ton, and you've carried them since the world started over."

And he had them, and she wanted them back. "How many tickets do you want for them?"

His brow arched. "You'd fuck for those books?"

"Volumes, *slaver*. And no. But I give great foot rubs and I'm happy to bet on chess. Your idiot brigade has not been able to beat me yet. And believe it or not, I've found three whole tickets while sweeping up at the end of the night. I'm rich!"

"Foot rubs?"

"Your mistake is thinking that all these men want is to get their dick wet." Of course they wanted that, but they *needed* so much more. Including verbal punishment she was happy to dole out.

Leaning closer, all lecher, he grinned. "Oh, I know what they want, sweetheart."

"Eww."

"Neil offered me three times your price. Came to my office with his hat in his hand. Fancies himself in love."

That deserved another eww, but Eugenia wasn't going to acknowledge how absurd the conversation had grown.

"And now I'm going to have to kill him for it." He set her arm free, watching her scowl. "You can't let these men fall in love with you. I don't have enough women to go around, and you're singlehandedly messing up the game by drawing them in with the virgin angle."

She couldn't help but feel a bit proud. But far more than proud, she felt disgusted. "So you're going to kill a man for wanting a woman? He doesn't even know me. And though he is handsome, he is not my type. Wait,"—maybe she had something to work with here—"could he afford me?"

"No. He'd be indentured for the next forty years."

Frowning, she asked the question no one had answered for her yet. "Exactly how much do I cost?"

"Aren't you going to beg for Neil's life?"

The whole idea was ridiculous. "You're not going to kill Neil. That would be stupid and a waste of a resource."

Deadpan, the captain said, "Twenty million."

As in tickets? "No woman on this boat has a quarter of that price! Why must you be such a dick?" And just to drive home her point, she picked up one of his pretty plates and smashed it on the ground. "And there is another five-thousand." And broke another one. "And there's another five-thousand. I might as well just break them all!"

Voice dropping, he warned, "Break another plate and I might just get mad."

"Twenty-million tickets at five-thousand tickets a fuck, is four-thousand fucks. One fuck every night of the year would take more than ten years to pay off! Don't look at me like that. Yes! I can do fucking math!" And *fucking math* should have been funny, considering the context. Normal Eugenia would have snorted. But nothing was normal. And nothing, not even air conditioning, was good. "Brooke is going to be out of your hellhole ship in two months, and you're telling me you think you deserve ten years of my life? YOU DON'T DESERVE ANY OF IT!"

"I like it when you wear your hair up." He tugged a tiny curl at her nape. "You look pretty."

"I *hate* you!"

Leaving with a chuckle, the door swung back and forth upon his exit—a panting, furious, sad, and all the other emotions Eugenia grinding her teeth in his wake.

***

After the ambush, shirking chores while her uterus sloughed off last month's cells, Eugenia stayed in her room until her period was over. When she emerged, tired of staring at the walls with nothing to do, and tired of not sleeping, she went to Joan and accepted the night's outfit.

Naughty nurse—chosen by the captain himself, no less.

At Table #2, staring at the white tablecloth she'd be washing later, resentment pinned her tongue to the roof of her mouth.

A hand landed on hers, shaking her out of the gloom. "All the new girls go through this. In a week or two, you'll be your old self again. Neil was a nice guy, but he knew better."

Dragging her eyes up took more effort than it should have. "What about Neil?"

The guest said it again. "He knew better."

But that would mean...

"Excuse me, I need to…" Inelegantly climbing from the cookie sheet, the lap, and over the other men in the way, she muttered, "use the ladies room."

Of course the captain was standing there, leaning against the wall. One leg crossed over the other as if he hadn't a care in the world. Tipping his chin, he greeted her, "Eugenia."

None of it made sense. None of it. "What if I had actually liked him?"

"Then I would have let you go."

Unsure why she was crying, especially where people could see, she said, "All he wanted was to hold a baby and be a daddy. He told me so six times at least!"

"And all you wanted was that one special guy to give your virginity to and live happily ever after."

Senseless murder because some schmuck fancied a woman who didn't like him back? "How could you?"

"You're unattainable. Three hundred men will grasp that now." Scratching his unshaven chin, he added, "Isn't that what you wanted?"

"Did he suffer?"

"No. Never saw it coming. I told him he could have you, then shot him in the head as he walked away. Happiest I've ever seen him."

There was no lie in it. Because as far as she had seen, neither of them had ever lied to one another. "I'm going to throw up."

Pushing open the door, he murmured, "Go on in then. Take the night off. I'll have Joan check on you later."

On her bed in her tiny, private room were both volumes of *Nelson's Textbook of Pediatrics*. Old friends she'd missed terribly. Old friends she fell asleep clutching to her chest as she curled up in the fetal position. Too tired to even climb under the blankets.

It was dark, late when the door opened and a weight sat at her side.

Warm hand landing on her hip, he sighed but said nothing. Did nothing but sit there with her, the sound of water lapping at the side of the ship.

"He wouldn't have made you happy."

Death grip on her textbooks, lashes salty from dried tears, Eugenia said nothing.

# Chapter Five

No stunt she pulled, public or private, could entice the captain to hit her again. To hurt her, to do something other than just *be around.* No matter how far she pushed or the damage she wrought, she couldn't get the bastard to raise his fist.

She broke every plate she could get her hands on in the kitchens.

He moved her to another portion of the boat, under guard, to make pottery. Which apparently the other ladies enjoyed and had failed to mention to the mentally unstable newcomer. The psychology was obvious. It was harder to break something she'd made, watched fired in a kiln, and held in her hands. But she did that too.

She'd slapped the captain right in the face in the middle of one of his dinner parties. Only for him to catch her hand and kiss her palm. Patting her on the rump, and he sent her back to Table #2.

When offerings began to show up outside her door, just like they did for the other women, Eugenia took the box of treasures and dumped it on the deck where that night's guests might see. Chapstick—something she confided to the other girls was a luxury she missed from before the bombs—a pretty green sweater, because air conditioning was divine but perfect when one had a cardigan. Hard candy, which she'd never mentioned nor did she care for. Perfume.

Eugenia had always hated perfume. But she had loved scented candles.

And one of those was in there too. It smelled of apples and crisp fall air. A three-wick beauty from a big chain store that had been popular for their soaps and bubble bath before they were blown off the map and the world had caught on fire.

That irreplaceable candle cracked against the deck; the glass-encased scented wax fractured just like her insides.

The last thing to flutter out of that box, unseen under all the crap a fool had thought to buy her with:

bruised wildflower petals some dope had carried in his pockets from God knew where to make this extra fancy.

Petals she crushed under her shoe as she glared at the gawking men waiting for their dinner and fuck time. And if that did not make her point strong enough, she spit on the pile of debris.

And still, the captain didn't strike her.

Though he did drag her away, a grip of steel about her nape. Led her to her tiny room and forced her to her knees.

At eye-level with his crotch, she snarled, "I swear to God I will bite it off if you whip it out!"

Was that actually heat in his face? Had she made him mad? Perfect.

"I don't want to fuck your mouth. I have Chloe to do that with a smile. Besides, I doubt you'd even know what to do with it."

His rotating, scheduled harem assignments meant nothing to her. The fact that next week she was on the board to service the captain in his private quarters was the stupidest gauntlet the man might have thrown down. “I’ve sucked cock, you prick. I can deepthroat like a goddamn champion. Just because I was a virgin, did you assume I’d never had a serious relationship? I was never a nun, though I keep waiting for you to whip up that outfit for me.”

“For Christ’s sake, Eugenia!”

“Stop leaving things in my room.” There it was. Said straight out. “You can’t buy me with textbooks and notepads. I don’t want your fucking reading lamp.”

Releasing her nape to take hold of her hair, the captain yanked until her back bowed and she struggled to hold his eyes. “I don’t need to buy you. I already own you.”

“What made you like this? It’s only been six years, and you must have been normal once. I’m not buying the lazy cowboy game you’re running! The murdering slaver who fails to partake with the men.”

His hand left her curls, palm trailing to cup her cheeks so his thumb might roughly trace her lips.

Pulling them in a way that was overly suggestive. "Sorry to disappoint, but I was always this way."

"Psychotic? There is medication for that, you know. I'm sure your raiding parties might still be able to find some. I'll make you a list and proper dosage. Better yet, grow some weed and roll a joint."

"You are something tonight, sugar. And this isn't just about the box a man *slaved* to prepare for you."

She hated when he found her amusing. Hated when he smiled. That fucking southern good ol' boy accent she hated most. "I'm not servicing you next week."

"But you just confessed that you possess the rare deepthroat skill."

"I'm not joking, Captain."

"I have told you twenty times, my name is Aaron."

"It's a stupid name."

"So is Eugenia."

"On that, we can agree." Knees aching, somehow having forgotten he still cupped her cheek, she pushed off his hand and climbed to her feet. "Take me off your schedule, or the acting out you've seen will be nothing compared to what I'll unleash. You should be shaking in your polished boots."

"Ten-thousand tickets a night for a game of chess and a foot rub."

"No."

"Fifty-thousand." He wasn't joking.

Which was ludicrous!

Gesturing wildly, because this was too crazy to hear, she shouted, "Have you actually lost your mind? You put me in your room and I find one sharp object, you're dead."

That earned a serial-killer smile. "Seventy-thousand."

"I don't understand how a man as clever as you has failed to realize that I am not interested in your company. Take those seventy-thousand hypothetical tickets and shove them up your ass. I'd rather fuck every man downstairs than touch your feet with my magic hands."

"Even John?"

Hmm. He had Eugenia there. "You might marginally outrank John, but don't take that as a compliment. He's scum. Not that you're not scum too. You are."

Laughing, the captain took a step back and leaned his weight on her dresser. "Chess and a foot rub. I'll even see you dressed in conservative clothes. The regular rules apply."

"You're only pushing this for show. You know I'm going to tell everyone you have a small dick and are terrible in bed."

Still chuckling, running a hand through his long, dark hair, he countered, "Tell them what you want. I don't care."

"A foot rub…" Negotiations of this level required pacing, leaving Eugenia bounding back and forth between her walls. "And one nightly game of chess. Standard clothes that cover all of me. And no sexual anything. Not even innuendo."

He had a dimple, one on full display with a cockeyed grin. "You still think you're going to find that one, forever guy?"

"I didn't get where I was because I let assholes like you make decisions for me. I'll get off your boat, and I'll find someone special. The whole world can't be like you."

Was that pity? "Eugenia, you'll find nothing better than this boat. It might take some time for you to figure that out, but you'll come to accept it."

Ignoring him, she went on. "And I'll keep breaking the shit they leave at my door. Let them spend their tickets on the others."

"Raoul has gathered intel on your preferences from the first night he saw you. Risked the wastes to hunt down things the other women told him you'd like. That's a bit coldhearted."

"Oh," she singsonged. "And then he falls in love and you kill him."

"Naw. He's had them all. The boys downstairs are running bets on who plows you first. He's got a lot of tickets riding on winning you with a box of crap."

How could she be so dense? "And that's why you're bribing me to come to your rooms."

"So what if I am?"

"You're worse than Wall Street… just without the slick suit or the manicured nails."

By God, he actually looked down at the grit under his fingertips as if it had never registered it before.

And she laughed at him.

And it felt good.

"You are hands down…"

Hazel eyes landed on hers, penetrating through her. Possessive, and creepy, and uninvited. "Hands down what?"

*That* she was not touching with a ten-foot pole. "I gotta get back to Table #2. Screw intellectualism. Who needs education and a functioning brain when they were born with tits and an ass?"

Brushing past her tormentor to escape, she almost crossed the threshold before he seized her hand and pulled her back. Pushing a tube of Chapstick against her palm, the captain closed her fingers around it. "Cherry flavored, your favorite."

Knowing by feel alone what was in her hand, she raised her eyes to his, and said, "I think I really will kill you next week."

Then she popped off the safety plastic and swiped it on her mouth. Smacking her lips once she recapped the tube and threw it right in his face. It bounced off his forehead and landed on her sheets. A corner of the room she had no intention of going near so long as a man was lurking, smirking, and disgustingly pleased.

So she flipped him off and turned.

At her back, he chuckled. “I’ll be thinking of your special skill while Chloe is sucking my cock later.”

Shouting down the hall, she countered, “I’ll give her some pointers before she comes up to your rooms.”

***

Up until it was her turn to *service the captain overnight*, the “trades” kept coming. One box outside her door even contained a live chicken.

What the fuck was she going to do with a chicken?

Not that she didn’t pick it up and pet it, finding the feathers soft and the animal willing.

Had it been a puppy, that man might have won the bets.

Human anatomy was one thing. Poultry was another. But they’d let her loose around knives in order to get chores done, and the pretty, cuddly bird was ended quickly.

A butcher's knife to the neck.

And just like wild game she caught back when she'd been free, she sat on the deck, looked over the view of a dead forest, and pulled the feathers so they might fall like snow. So she might have some repetitive action to distract her while she looked upon a world that had failed everyone in a way.

The bird was roasted and served to her table, set down in a bed of potatoes and carrots. The head served alongside. She didn't eat a bite.

"I really did think the chicken might have won you." It was Malachi who laughed, patting his full belly. "Think of the eggs. You could have traded those for more tickets."

"I live in a closet and have nothing to feed it." And yeah, she did feel a bit bad for killing the poor, aromatic thing.

"Of course you do! The other girls live in multi-room suites. Much nicer than the bunks we share downstairs." Nudging the guy at his side, he said, "Right, Verne? You and I both know Jessica's room well."

"How much does that cost?" Because this was fascinating information.

"Oh, twenty-five thousand tickets a night! But it's a real bed, not a pallet. And there is a private toilet and a soft woman."

Jessica was nice. Quiet, disassociated. Kept to herself. Wasn't the kind to put broken glass in the new girl's food.

Someone deserving of a fine room to rest in, considering the shit she had to put up with.

"I like her." Which should be said. "Jessica's cool."

The men at the table toasted Jessica's name. Clicked their glasses and shared a moment of comradery Eugenia knew better than to analyze.

And then she saw *him* watching her.

Because this was his night to "win" the bets. She'd be in his rooms for a week, and he wanted every man here to know it. So he'd hold the prize. So he'd run the money.

Dirtbag.

A dirtbag who came to collect her when the bell was rung and the men lined up to dump their food and drink on Scarlett and Kim.

Where everyone could hear, he said, "We struck a deal, siren. Come along now, and let's discuss that deepthroat you claimed to be an expert at performing."

He led her away by the hand, wrapping an arm around her middle, as she hissed, "I'd throw myself off the side of this boat before I'd take your sorry penis in my mouth." She was tempted to do it at that moment. Which was precisely why he'd put that covetous arm around her waist. "How many women have jumped overboard?"

His reply was easy. "I haven't lost one yet. In fact, all those who leave always come back."

"Bullshit."

But Joan. Nice—as much as Eugenia hated to admit it—helpful, accommodating Joan had come back.

Brooke would be leaving after ten more men fucked her. Something she might accomplish in as little as three days. And no way was that girl ever coming back to this place. Not when she'd worked so hard to earn her way off.

Eugenia couldn't wait to see her go, to wave and well wish, and taste a bit of freedom she'd never earn. At least not with tickets and whoring.

# Chapter Six

The captain's rooms were…

Much nicer than hers. Music came from an AI in the corner, *Alecia*. A device Eugenia had not seen in six years. A bit of hoarded history not one of the women had mentioned when they gathered for breakfast to poke fun at her turn.

And she'd thought she'd heard it all. His sexual preferences—hard, fast, from behind. His tendencies to brood if he wasn't in the mood or the girl talked too much. Captain's competitiveness at games and the way he refused to touch after sex.

The women were allowed to sleep on the bed, at a distance, but most chose the couch after it was over.

And he never, ever ejaculated inside. Same rules on the deck. The ol' pull out and pray method.

Despite Eugenia's lack of interest, they had given her a primer on the animal.

*Manus dickus assholeus.*

The music though…

"Hold on for a moment, eh?" Her smile dropped as he pulled her inside. Eugenia had not heard pre-bomb music in so long it felt like stepping on the moon.

"I had a feeling you'd like PJ Harvey."

Stricken, she listened, memories flooding in of campfires and lovers. Marshmallows and making out in their tent. The ground shaking to this exact song when the world ended as she climaxed from some extremely satisfying sixty-nineing.

But the ground kept shaking, and the camping party figured it had to be Mt. Saint Helen.

Not nuclear war.

There was cell signal enough to listen to the screams of newscasters as more cities blew apart. And then there was the quiet of the woods.

Which were not quiet at all. They were deafeningly loud.

Her entire family was gone, and they wouldn't have wanted their brilliant daughter braving radiation to pick through garbage for their corpses.

Not pragmatic Mom and Dad. He worked for NASA; she was a brain surgeon.

And this was the last song Eugenia heard when almost everyone who mattered to her was obliterated in radioactive ash. The song—had the world not shaken with such force that they were knocked apart—she suspected Li Wei intended to propose to her once they'd caught their breaths and shared a long kiss.

She'd seen the ring in his pack. The simple band and inset diamonds—exactly to her taste. Something she could wear under surgical gloves. He knew her so well, treated her with respect.

Was willing to move against his family's hesitations despite the fact that she was not Chinese.

Eugenia was ecstatic to accept. All of their future planned out after graduation. He'd run a family practice. She'd further her education until ready to specialize in pediatric surgery.

But his beloved family was in one direction and hers was in another.

And everyone died.

*Stories from the City, Stories from the Sea.*

And how did the bastard Captain know the power of this song?

How could he be so cruel?

Playing that warbling, beautiful, aggressive songstress. Eugenia's guts would have spilled out all over the floor. Fortunately, they were held tight by a conservative, cotton summer dress.

Steering her toward a set of damask sofas, facing one another as if they were on the fucking *Titanic*, the captain offered, "There's wine."

"Yeah." Wine would be good, a whole fucking bottle.

Li Wei had been so handsome, so smart, so kind. Suave yet funny. Perfect. A sharp dresser yet not pretentious like his parents… or hers.

Sitting on that couch, Eugenia swallowed the full cup of Bordeaux in three gulps.

All of this witnessed by the man mirroring her seat on the opposite couch. A man to whom she'd never lied, and who had never lied to her.

A man waiting for an explanation for the look on her face.

"I would have said yes… to this song. I would have said yes, had a wedding, saved children's lives on the operating table, maybe even had one of my own. But the ground started shaking, and he forgot to ask in the chaos. I don't know what happened to the ring. Maybe still at the campsite?"

"Did you want a boy or a girl?"

This was too much to bear. Grief hard enough, and anger far more comforting. "Why the fuck are you playing PJ Harvey?"

"Because you hum her songs while you work."

"I do not!" Humming was for suckers and fools who thought there was a happy ending in this shit place.

"*Alecia*, play Arcade Fire."

And the torture ended, the captain refilling her glass.

She sipped the second round, accepting that every last survivor had some kind of PTSD, and unfortunately hers had been witnessed by someone who'd use it against her.

A man she knew hated small talk during his scheduled sex sessions. So small talk it would be. "I saw Arcade Fire live when I was seventeen. Lied to my parents and snuck out. Got a wristband to buy beer and sat on the shoulders of some bruiser whose name I don't remember. Small venue, but the best show I'd ever seen."

Lifting his glass, the captain saluted her. "My favorite was MUSE, the *Simulation Theory* tour."

"Oh... that was a good one." No argument there.

Li Wei had stood at her back, cuddling as they rocked to the music. As they marveled at the monster when it burst out over the stage. Both of them drunk on Goose IPA.

"What was his name?"

"None of your business." Truly and deeply. Abso-fucking-lutely none of his business.

"So you weren't looking for *the one*. You already had him."

"The fact that you think I might reduce my happiness to the outdated concept of *the one* goes to show how little you know me."

That earned a smirk. "Did you just call me old?"

"You are old." Maybe not old enough to have fathered her, but still old.

"And you are very young." Followed with another raised glass and a devilish grin.

"But I won't be your brand of young in ten years, assuming I fuck one of your men every night."

"You never answered. Boy or girl?"

Okay, maybe small talk wasn't working.

Standing, wine glass in hand, she left the couch and the game of twenty questions to poke around his room—touching everything in an effort to annoy him. To feel. To remember regular things.

There were so many colors.

She had not realized how her blank walls and pale sheets were so lacking.

Reds, purples, the green of living plants that were no more.

Fortifying herself with another sip of honest to God wine, she turned, feeling a real skirt swish around her knees, and decided to wrap it up. "Where are you going to do it?"

How indulged he looked. Every bit the pirate king on his stolen throne. "Do what, Eugenia?"

"Rub my feet. As per our agreement."

And he laughed again, understanding he'd lost her word game. Setting down his glass on a pristine coffee table, standing to remind her how much larger he was.

The jaw, the cheekbones, the lips, the hair.

Rouge pirate through and through.

"Anywhere you want it."

Considering all the fun she might have at his expense if he played along, she batted her eyelashes. "Anywhere?"

Yet he was already there, toying with curls Joan had spent ages battling into submission for Eugenia's *special night*. "Right here will do."

"You said I got to pick." It was a half-complaint as he brought them both down to soft carpet.

Thumb pads to her insoles, he said, "You took too long."

Jesus Christ was he either gifted with fingers from the gods, or she was literally that in need of human touch. Groaning, her head fell back.

For an hour, she endured the best foot rub known to womankind. Utterly brazen in her groans, happy enough to fall asleep on soft, clean carpet.

Distraught to wake in a strange bed, the arm and leg of a man she hated weighing her down.

*Breaking his own rules*, because where their feet tangled, her skin was bare.

Since the sun was up, her duty was done, and she didn't have to stand for this. Moving out of his arms, she scampered for the door—the unlocked door—like a complete coward.

***

"Did he do that tongue thing?"

Noodles today. Handmade by Chloe, the same woman who struck up a conversation all the other women must have all shared in the past.

"No." Eugenia didn't have a thing for the rugged, evil type who traded in human currency.

"Please, sweetie, you don't have to pretend here. We've all fucked him dozens of times. The first time, you always get the tongue thing. A glass of wine. What music did he have on?"

"PJ Harvey."

Slurping up a noodle, Chloe asked, "Who's that?"

"It doesn't matter." And it didn't. It never would again.

Prepping another bite of good noodles in bad broth, Chloe said, "Just do the week. Let him tie you up if that makes it easier. Let him fuck you a little too hard. And move on. It's only six more days."

"You have got to fucking be kidding me..." Bondage was his thing? How cliché for a pirate.

"He really didn't fuck you." And the whole table, Joan included, stared.

"Oh, we fucked all night. So much fucking. Didn't you see me walking funny?"

"Jesus, are you in for it, kid." Pink-cheeked and teasing, Chloe added, "I'd bet tickets he's breaking you in. Considering the size of his uncut cock, he probably needs to. No reason to damage the merchandise."

Which wasn't funny at all.

"You know I'm joking, right? I mean about the damage part. We all agree, and he keeps a tally if we're willing to take that beast the old--fashioned way or down the throat. A little lube, a little *wine*, and he'll get it in. Brace, think of England, and let him finish."

"That is… extremely unsettling. Especially as you are not British."

Chloe shrugged a pretty, uncovered shoulder. "Britain is gone. As is Japan, the Philippines, South

Africa, Alaska… The only way out of this is getting to the Pacific and finding a sailboat to Russia."

Scientifically speaking, the woman was spot on. The heat melted ice, exposing fertile land. A person just had to cross a radioactive ocean, pay the mafia, sail thousands of miles, and show up old and ready to die.

"Six more nights, and then I won't have to go back again for at least a handful of months."

It was the quietest of the women, a practical girl, who asked, "Don't you like it in there?"

"I liked medical school and my fiancé and my future. No, the fact that he plays music and rubbed my feet doesn't cut it."

In chorus, the entire fucking room erupted. "*He rubbed your feet?*"

"Don't think he did it out of some kind of… whatever. I outplayed him in a word game. That's all."

And with that one flippant reply, half the room turned frostier than a glacier; the other kept staring down at their noodles.

They couldn't possibly be jealous? "I didn't fuck him."

"You should have! Now it's going to be so much harder for the rest of us!" Brooke—Brooke, who was days away from earning her freedom—shouted.

"I'm sorry?" Not that Eugenia was, but what on earth was someone to say to that?

"Just let him have sex with you. No more of this Joan of Arc shit. We are tired of trying to live up to your crusade! None of us want to whore, all right?"

"You have a choice in who you let into your bodies! Like me, you can refuse."

The quiet one again, Jessica. "I've been here three years. What do you know?"

"I know that he's told me my debt is twenty-million, and that I would not be able to fuck my way out of that hole even if I tried."

And that shut up the table but did not stop the squinty-eyed consideration of Joan.

# Chapter Seven

There was no music on night two. But there was more wine.

“The girls told me you were going to tie me up and fuck too hard.” She raised her glass but refused to drink. “Apparently, you also have a large penis. I'd love to know how many tickets it cost you to bribe them into making that comment.”

Clinking her glass and taking a sip of burgundy, he asked, “Do you like large dicks?”

“No. I like nice men.”

Hand scrubbing a stubble-free cheek, he said, “Then you’ll be disappointed.”

“You shaved… and you’re dressed practically in a suit. Couldn’t find the jacket?”

That caught him, right with his palm to his outstretched neck.

And the moment was too good to pass up. Eugenia slid closer to stroke where his shirt sleeves were rolled up and a muscular forearm was on display. “And look how pretty you are in a white button-down and slacks. I’ll tell you what, sugar. One fuck for a scented candle, some Chapstick, and five-thousand tickets? I’ll even throw in some foreplay, wine, and music before I grease up the ol’ strap-on and I work it in.”

Her game backfired when he caught up a handful of hair and held it to his nose. “You know why foreplay is not allowed.”

Looking from side to side, night two of the grandeur of the captain’s apartments was far less impressive. “But it happens here. I’ve heard all about that thing you do with your tongue, *you dirty slut*.”

Smirking, melting into her teasing, muscular chest on display where he failed to do up the last buttons, and disgustingly brazen, he hummed. “Consider it a perk of leadership.”

"Used goods aren't really my style." She looked down to his tented slacks.

He bantered right back. "Two virgins does not a good sexual experience make."

On that, he was wrong. She'd had plenty of intensely fulfilling sexual experiences with Li Wei. "Sounds like your first time was a bit underwhelming. And not that I'm ever discussing my sexual history with you, but you seem smart enough to grasp that there are a lot of creative things partners can enjoy that don't involve penetration. Considering that you're basically a pimp, I'd have expected you'd do more than doggie style night in and night out. You've made sex a chore for all parties involved."

The smile he gave her was legendary. "Well, well, the women *have* been talking."

Taking her first sip of wine, she followed with, "Apparently, you're uncircumcised. I commend your parents. I think it's a barbaric practice."

He mirrored her sip. "What else did they tell you?"

With a sigh, she took her place on the couch, legs crossed at the knee—a thing her mother would have corrected at once. Ladies cross their legs at the ankle. And stretched back against the pillows until her face pointed up at the ceiling. "Between you and me, I think two or three of them are sweet on you. The rest are angry with me for not fucking you. Unfortunately, they didn't believe it when I lacked the details. You should have prepared me with a speech. The bondage fetish would have been useful to know."

Unlike the previous night, he left his couch to plop down at her side. "Are you asking me to tie you up?"

"No, thank you." If his sitting so near was some kind of test, she was not going to scoot. Not when they had an agreement. "Repetitive doggy style also sounds extremely boring." Head lolling so her gaze might leave the ceiling and meet his, she asked, "It must be, right? Why not change it up. Laziness? Disinterest? Don't take this as a compliment, but the man who came up with all these twisted rules that make up the society on this ship… his lack of sexual creativity is a bit disappointing."

"They did mention that tongue thing. Is that earning me any credit?"

She should not have laughed, couldn't even blame it on the wine. But it was funny that this man just refused to be insulted by fact. "You should be gentler with them. Maybe assist in their climax if you're going to get your own. Aren't pirates supposed to be sexy and wicked in bed?"

From playful to disapproving, he took away her glass and set it down. "As cute as your game is, their time in this room isn't about pleasure, and you know that."

"They did mention that you pull out long before climax and finish yourself, with a towel ready and everything so none of your semen gets on them. And if the girl wants, she can give you head instead of fucking for the same amount of tickets. That's how they try to impress you. Because I think we both know you're bored of the game you created."

"If I don't treat them equally, it upsets the status quo." And he looked broody when he said it, just the way the women described.

What had been intended to annoy him was actually far more interesting than she expected. "Equally selfish in bed except for the occasional tongue thing? I don't fuck anyone, and it seems your rules haven't suffered too much for it."

"Only Neil."

*Ouch.* How could she have forgotten this man murdered someone for nothing more than asking to pay off her debt?

The room suddenly chilly, she stopped lazing and sat up like a proper lady. Legs crossed at the ankle and shoulders straight. "Tell me in detail how I'm supposed to describe our night to the women over breakfast. You can have your status quo. I don't care if every last soul on this boat thinks I fucked you. Win the pot of tickets. Recycle it into your economy. Did we do it on the bed? On the sofa? Are you a floor kinda guy?"

"Against the wall." He nodded his chin to a dark corner. "Face-to-face so I could see you. Everyone will expect that for your first time."

"Did I come?"

"Would you be able to describe it?"

"No…" Eugenia wouldn't be able to climax if there wasn't some emotional connection. "That's not a lie I'd be able to pull off."

"And now you understand why the men dump their food and beer on the same women they kill themselves to buy. Can't have the natural female physiological response kick in. There can't be any ties—why the women don't cry but some of the men do when the door closes and the night's entertainment is over."

"You are a really sick man." A sick man who had put his hand on her knee.

Who was lifting that hand to pinch her chin as if he might kiss her. "I would be gentle with you, if I could trust you not to breathe a word of it."

Cocking a brow, she asked, “And what about that natural female physiological response?”

Lips cocked, hazel eyes languid, he said, “You hate me. I don’t think we have a problem there.”

“Which brings us full circle to why on earth you think I’d want your dick inside me.”

“Because we’d both like it, and you know that.”

She brushed her lips over his, not a kiss. A taunt. “But I’m the unattainable whore.”

“Eugenia.” The warning in his voice was unmistakable.

“I’ll tell everyone you fucked me in the corner, standing, face-to-face. You came on my stomach, wiped yourself off on my dress. I cried after and slept on the couch.”

“You’ll need to smear some blood on your skirt.” Serious as murder, he added, “I am big. You’ll bleed the first few times.”

"And after five more nights of charming conversation, the other women on weekly rotation, I'll only have to play this game three or so times a year." Which sounded so ugly to say out loud. "I should just throw myself overboard right now."

Pinching the bridge of his nose, he leaned back against the seat and shut his eyes.

Blood on the dress wasn't going to be enough. "You're going to need to slap me around a little. And you'll need a scratch or two, because I would have fought back."

"It doesn't have to be this way." How dare he look angry? How dare he make this out as if she were the difficult one?

"I'm just following your rules, *maintaining your status quo*. Don't get mad at me if you don't like living in the hell you created."

Standing, he towered over her to snarl, "But at least I'm living. And so are you. And so is every other fucking person on this boat! They are all *safe*."

"Temper, temper, slaver. Use it. Hit me now before you puss out."

And he did, catching her when she flew at him on a roar and fought back like a wildcat. The tussle was short-lived—but effective. Pinned to the ground, her hands caught above her head, bleeding strips where nails had raked him decorated all the way from his neck to where his shirt exposed too much chest for the costume to be considered gentlemanly. Marks that would scab and sit on display for others to see.

"Jesus, Eugenia…" He panted, hard against her leg.

Chest rising and falling, hungry for more violence but subdued no matter how hard she struggled, she forced herself still. "You need to get off me now."

"I don't want to." Which, of course he didn't. Not with a massive erection pressed to her thigh.

Which was problematic. This was supposed to be a charade, but he was leaning in close, and there was nowhere to retreat when one was already caught.

Lips to her jaw, not quite kissing, more like a man desperate for air, he pleaded, "Five-hundred thousand tickets."

"You can't buy me, Aaron. How many times do I have to tell you that? I am not for sale."

"Then fuck me because you want to!" His grip on her wrists tightened. Muscles bulging to stretch the fabric of his shirt and he tensed. "We both know you are as wet as I am hard. Hate-fuck me, scratch me to bits, *but let me inside you*."

His hand was already bunching up her skirt as if she'd given permission. Eugenia snarled, "Have you lost your mind?"

Leaning up with a sexy smirk, one that belied eyes dark with passion, he teased, "I'll do the tongue thing."

Afraid his hand might reach higher than midthigh, that she might be forced to face something she didn't dare think of, she whispered, "My answer is no."

"Fuck." And he was off her, running a hand through his hair as he paced.

Stopping only long enough to see where she lay on the floor, skirt halfway up, disheveled, half warrior and completely agitated. The image of her laid out like a sacrifice caught him. Caught him dead in his tracks from whatever mental gymnastics he was working through to get his way.

Jaw tense, he ordered, "You sleep on the bed. I'll take the couch."

Which was so utterly backward she didn't know where to begin. But she did not argue. Not when he looked like that. Not when he was looking at her *that way*.

"You're going to be under guard when I'm not around. Suicide risk. Everyone will expect it."

He wasn't entirely wrong. Had he really raped her, the mind might have gone someplace too dark despite her desire to survive. So she nodded.

"Get to bed. I'm going to go jack off in the shower."

No need to tell her twice, she scampered from the floor and dove under the covers. She heard the water running and knew she'd never fall asleep.

But he took forever. And it had been a long day. Long months. A long six years.

Her eyes closed. And when she woke, she slipped from under the covers, the man snoring on the couch awake the instant her foot hit the ground.

"Aren't you forgetting something?"

Hand to the latch, not quite awake but very eager to be gone, she turned her head to see if she'd left an item in the room.

And then he was there, his hand on her hand, pulling her touch from the latch. Slowly turning her until her back hit the panel.

As close to her as he had been when they wrestled on the floor. As close as they would have been had he actually fucked her against the wall.

Then he took her chin to inspect the light bruise on her cheek. Eugenia found she could not meet his eyes, though she felt his silent demand she do so.

When he won—she the coward and he the clear victor—softly, he said, "There's no blood on your dress."

"Maybe you're not as big as you think you are." She wasn't even trying to banter; she just wanted out of the room and in the safety of her own.

"I am."

"Listen. I have chores—"

"Turn around. Trust me."

She'd trust a venomous snake before she trusted the slaver, but still, she turned, felt the weight of his body press her to the door. As if he needed a moment to collect himself.

As if he enjoyed the feel of her.

And then he lifted her skirt before she might stop him. And spit. Rubbing it into her thigh with the fabric.

While she tried to stop her heart from racing.

While she could feel him reach into his trousers and rub himself. While he worked his shaft and groaned against her neck. The sharp sting when his lips locked on her throat and he sucked hard enough to leave a mark. The vulgar sound he made when he came on the backs of her thighs.

And once again rubbed his fluids clean with her skirt.

Breathless, he spun her around before her hand might find the knob, caught the look in her eyes. "One more thing."

Hooking her bodice, he tore, buttons flying until heaving cleavage was on display. Eugenia pressing so hard against the door she might as well have merged atoms with the wood.

Taking in his work, he sighed. "Now they will believe it. Go to breakfast just like this. Wear the dress all day. Say it was punishment for scratching."

This was so much more than just spreading a rumor. This was a public shaming.

"Don't cry. It's not real, remember?"

But it felt real, and her eyes did sting. Because her pride had always been on the large side, and this was humiliating.

# Chapter Eight

The captain was right, she didn't need to tell their concocted story. One look at her semen-stained dress, at the spot of blood where he must have bitten himself before he spit, at the torn bodice and her exposed cleavage...

One look told it all.

Or maybe it was her unnatural silence, her *deer in the headlights* unblinking stare.

She did her chores in that dress, sweating under so much fabric. She ate her meals in that dress, the other ladies kind enough to not poke fun or ask questions.

She worked Table #2 in that dress. The only table to which she had ever been assigned, and she knew why. Because he had his usual spot, where he could look right at her. Listen in on all she said.

Keep tabs.

Just like the three guys who now followed her everywhere she went as she scrubbed floors or washed dishes. And though Eugenia recognized them, she couldn't remember their names.

They didn't talk to her anyway. They talked to each other as they guarded the commodity that just might be tempted to jump overboard. Talk, it seemed, was their other job. Spread the tale of how the pretentious virgin had fallen.

How all the men snickered when the captain strode by, her scratches on his neck and chest. His hair tied back so they could not be missed.

Jumping at every noise in a party that was nothing but noise, one of her evening guests said, "We know he can be a little rough. And for your first time, that was probably a lot to handle. I'd treat you right, if you let me come to your room. Show you how it's supposed to be between a girl and a man."

"Woman." When was she going to get it through these *boys'* heads that they were women?

"I stand corrected. Between a woman and a man." And his smile was kind, the gray at his temples charming, considering.

And what was there to say except, "I'm sore."

Nodding in understanding, he said, "We'll talk about it again in a week or two. There's no rush."

No rush, because not one of them believed she'd ever leave the boat. "Would you like to play another round of chess?"

Which she would win, because she always won. The tri-state chess champion. Full ride to Harvard Med. From a prestigious WASP family of scientists, dripping in privilege. Who'd been given her first strand of pearls at her sweet sixteen.

Who met and fell in love with Li Wei at a lecture on anatomy, pickled corpse between them. Li Wei, who went after his family when she begged him not to go near the radiation.

Who was dead now, by one means or another.

Everyone was dead. And those who were alive traded carnival tickets for sexual favors and a chance to play chess with a *girl* in a blue cotton summer dress covered in dried come. The torn, conservative outfit far more humiliating than any of the stripper costumes the women rotated between them.

A *girl* who had a job, and that job was to engage with the *guests*. "Were you married… before?"

"Aye, with five kids, if you can believe it." The older gentlemen, unlike the younger, did like to look back with a smile.

"I wanted to be a pediatric surgeon. Was in my second year of Harvard Med. I like kids."

"Yeah? We all pegged you as a bookworm."

That earned a half-hearted chuckle. "Sure. Textbooks. The more graphic the better. Show me a broken femur and the pins and screws that hold it back together any day."

"You must find us boring." And clearly she'd embarrassed him, the older man blushing as he made a poor move on the board.

"No." And that was true. None of them were boring, not that many of them weren't totally disgusting. "For example, I think you're nice. I think Gus could use more soap. I think Benji's jokes are vulgar, and I like the way François says my name. *Eugenia*." She took his queen, basically ending the game, though it would take him ten more moves to realize it. "I'm a lot of things, but bored isn't one of them."

"Angry?"

"Yes."

"I can understand that too. Five kids, remember?"

"And a wife."

"I can't think about her..." Because by the shadow crossing his face, it hurt too much.

She understood that too, but had always been a glutton for punishment, it would seem. "His name was Le Wei. I think about him. And how fucking stupid he was for going straight to Boston instead of listening to me. His family was dead. My family was dead. Everyone was dead. And he was a fucking medical student who knew exactly what that level of radiation would do to a human body."

"Yeah, well, us guys have never been too good on the listening part."

"I think he wanted to die. I think a lot of people—right after it happened—couldn't handle what they knew the world would become."

"You seem like you're doing all right."

She took another piece. A rook. "I'm about five minutes away from throwing myself over the side of that railing. Headfirst, because I know that, from this height, my neck will break on impact."

Eugenia didn't mean it. She couldn't have. But it felt like exactly what should have been said. And maybe even what she should have done. But she never would. Too stubborn and with too many scores to settle first.

"Did you hear my news?" Brooke was nothing but grins as she rushed up and threw her arms around a startled, unexpecting Eugenia. “Tomorrow, I get to disembark. Early, thanks to you.”

“Oh! Wow.” Were her eyes stinging again? “That’s wonderful. Really? Congratulations. I’ll be there to cheer you on.”

“I’m going to go south. Just like you suggested, so the winter’s aren't so cold.”

Well, that was how geography typically worked, but the distance she’d have to walk to reach it would take months. “Stay away from City. Or outposts with weapons. Small farming communities always need an extra pair of hands. Do you have a compass? A map?”

But Brooke wasn’t listening, already moving to the next girl to rejoice in her freedom.

“Don’t trust anyone!” Eugenia shouted over the party’s din. “Don’t stop to help anyone! Never stop!”

“You’re going to get in trouble if you keep that up. He’s already looking,” her chess partner warned. Gesturing to her cheek, to her bruise, he whispered, "And I'd rather not see you with another one of these."

"You're right." And he was. Utterly correct across the board. "What do I know? I'm just whoring myself out on a boat. Clearly, I have no idea what the fuck I'm talking about."

"Would you like a drink? On the house."

"Yes. And if you're willing to give me two, I'll let you win this game." On the edge of hysterics, not even sure what was making her hyperventilate, she wiped at her cheek. It was wet. "You can brag to all the guys how you beat me."

"In that case, I'll give you three. But no one else gets to win for at least a month."

"It's a deal."

That was the game on the ship after all. Deals, tickets, pretty Korean-American girls who got to leave and who should not go south… or north… or east… or west. Because the entire world was a fucking nightmare, and she only had one thing to trade.

Three beers did help. And her chess partner beat her in a show that drew a crowd to cheer for his victory.

When she went to the captain's room for the third night, he was waiting. Tub full in his massive bathroom. A clean set of pajamas—his pajamas—waiting. A fluffy towel too, shampoo, conditioner for curly hair. A bar of hand-milled soap from a fancy pre-bombs boutique.

And zero conversation.

Though he did watch her bathe. Not that she so much as noticed he was in the room.

He didn't gain her attention until he took her to bed, pulling her close—arm and leg draped over her body. Which was utterly against the rules, as she was covered from throat to ankles.

Held a little too tightly, she slept with him. Woke with him. Dressed with him.

And even stood next to him when Brooke disembarked. Something special in the woman's pack

Eugenia had asked for in the awkward morning hours.

"When you found my pack. Did you keep the map inside?"

"Yes."

"I want to give it to Brooke." She failed to add why. There isn't much drinkable water around here, and if Brooke didn't know where to find it, she'd die all the sooner.

The captain had granted her request. No tickets required.

A map that had cost Eugenia an astounding amount of trade. A map where the ship floated on a dirty lake in no man's land.

One she'd given to a giddy and distracted Brooke, hugging her so hard the petite thing squealed. And then left with a grin, waving as the ladies cheered and some of the men cried.

"She looks too clean and too healthy." It had to be said. And it seemed a fair question for the maker of rules and giver of pajamas. “What happens when she tells someone we’re here?”

It wasn’t unkind, but it was unsettling. “No one ever tells. Not when they see what the world is really like out there.”

“As if you’d know.” The captain had been running his kingdom. She’d been the one on the outside.

“Then tell me about it tonight.”

Oh, she’d tell him, tell him all the ugly. “You won’t like anything I have to say.”

But he did listen to her say it. How she had tried for the first two years to find a town with a doctor who needed an assistant. How the men just acted like beasts. The times she’d been caught, the ways she’d escaped. The lives she’d taken with surgical precision, because everyone underestimated a pretty, young redhead.

“And John, tell me about him.”

“Found him lost on the side of the road. Thirsty. It’s easier to avoid the dogs in a larger party, so I gave him some water. He thought we should fuck in all the downtime. One knee to the crotch ended that. And then we discussed the map, always trying to get us closer to City. I would never have come this way if I'd known you were here." And that map had been fucking expensive. Whatever the captain did to keep knowledge of his creepy oasis out of the mouths of City, it worked.

"I'll answer that unspoken question." The man looking too goddamn proud of himself. "We watch the roads. Kill those who don't pass muster. Stage the bodies along the way. We knew you were coming about twenty miles up. I watched you myself, carrying that ridiculous backpack of textbooks. Had the lights turned on for you and everything."

A welcome home? To know it had all been staged was so unsettling. "And because there was a woman in that party of two, you didn't just approach or attack."

"Transition is easier if you come to us."

"Was John in on it all along?"

"No. He tried to sell you fair and square." The man looked down at his nails. Nails far cleaner than they had been that first night. "And fair and square, I cut out his tongue. I don't mind the occasional over-exaggeration, but repetitive lying is against ship's rules."

For some reason, that sparked an unwanted yet comforting sense of justice. "Because he bragged to the men about what a great ride I'd been?"

"That's not all he said…"

"How many tickets buys his freedom?"

"One-hundred thousand." The captain held up his hands at her gape. "Now, before you start screaming, hear me out. The men never save enough. They spend it all coming upstairs. No one leaves the ship, not when the life I offer here is better than anything they'd find out there."

He knew just how to chill her, how to work her nerves. "Brooke left this morning."

Nodding, he concurred. "And Brooke will be back. The lights will be on for her when she comes home. A clean room and a hearty meal. A shoulder to cry on."

Brooke wouldn't be back. Not when all she worked for was the ability to get off this horrible ship. "You really do underestimate us, don't you?"

His voice grew soft when he said, "You never ask me personal questions. What are you afraid to learn, Eugenia?"

Rising to the challenge, a red eyebrow cocked, an unfriendly tone to her query. "Personally, I'd like to know—how long do you think it's going to take me to find a way off this boat?"

"Redheaded siren." He grinned, leaning back to sip his wine. "We both know you're never getting off my boat. You have it good here, and eventually, you'll accept that."

"I really do hate you." With every last fiber of her being.

"You *hate* being wrong. You're terrible at accepting change. You led a spoiled, tunnel-vision life, where you worked hard and achieved remarkable things. Where you could only imagine one version of yourself, and anything different was inconceivable."

This was how she knew he was insane. "Yeah, a whore is a great job when I could have been a surgeon. You got me. The complete loss of equality has been just dandy. Oh, the violence? Peachy! Sexual assault… it's exactly what every girl dreams of."

"You're cute when you're angry." The way he said it, his eyes aglow… was dangerous.

"I'm always angry."

"And you're always beautiful."

# Chapter Nine

She had not kissed him, had absolutely not invited the attention, but when the captain pulled her to his chest that night—the big spoon to her little spoon—he'd taken advantage of the bared skin and a manipulation of the rules.

This man didn't cuddle. All the women who endured his cock were very clear on that point.

Which Eugenia had no issue of reminding him.

If they didn't have to do it, she shouldn't have to either.

Leaving him laughing despite her struggles and complaints.

Soft kisses on her neck, the gentle suction of her earlobe. Murmurs of all the things he wanted to do to her body... and not one of them involved doggie style.

Unleashed, he was utterly filthy, left her shivering as she tried to ignore rasping words. As she tried not to remember how good some of those things he'd spoken of had felt long ago when the world was normal.

There was no talk of price. Only a swirling tongue in the shell of her ear.

Only a powerful embrace she stood no chance of escaping.

Only the heat of a heavy member against the mound of her ass. The murmurs of a man gently undulating against her, his voice thicker than honey.

"Foreplay is against the rules!" Every bit of his game was unacceptable.

Nipping her earlobe, he asked, "Would you consider this foreplay?"

Yes! Who wouldn't? Her nipples were hard, her body reactive. She was only human, for crying out loud. "I'm *not* having sex with you."

"Precisely. So it's not foreplay. It's just play. And there are no rules about that." Dark chuckles, dragging his tongue up the column of her throat in a languid wipe. "And even if there were, I'd break them... and you'd never tell."

Oh, fuck that! She'd scream it to the dinner party. "Is this the same line you give all the women forced to whore on your ship? Same tripe you fed Kim when it was her turn to tolerate this last week? I bet she blew you to keep it short and slept on the couch."

That earned a bite on the shoulder he'd just exposed. "As much as I'd love for you to be jealous, we both know you're not. Don't spoil my fun by reminding me."

"It's not sustainable, Aaron. The ship's culture, the women, the men, the lack of *orgasm* in the sense that family units are required for a future to develop. Workers will eventually grow old. This culture will fail. There will be a mutiny." And she said all of that out loud, squirming and sighing under his lips on her skin. "Please stop doing that. It's distracting."

Groaning, the warmth of his voice moving from his chest straight to her nipples, he ran his lips back to her ear. "Slip your hand between your thighs and tell me what you feel like." It wasn't a question, and it should not have left her on the verge of coming undone. "Eugenia, touch yourself like you do in your room. When no one is looking and you take what you need. When you're thinking of me."

She would not moan. She would not!

But he knew how to strum up a response. "You'll be thinking of me next time you do it. Thinking of this." Rocking his hips against her backside, his erection just as large as she had been warned.

"Is this the famous tongue thing?" she panted.

Another wicked laugh. "No. I've never touched any of them like this and you know that."

"I'm just a better opponent." Breathless, hating herself a little for indulging. "And since violence didn't work, you think seduction will."

Turning her chin, lips brushing hers, he said, "If I thought seduction would work, I'd be inside you right now."

"Psychological warfare then?"

Hazel eyes sparkled. "Do you feel outmatched? Does it feel good to know I want you?"

Good wasn't a word worthy of how she felt. She felt depraved… and liked it.

She liked it for hours. Melting into a puddle of contentment as he bent the rules.

When he moved to her feet and sucked her toe into his mouth, the gush of wetness between her legs was something she was never going to admit to herself. Just as she'd never speak of how loudly she moaned.

***

There was one more night with the captain: of squabbles, debate, petty insults, laughter, and Eugenia refusing to sleep with him no matter how he laughed and the exorbitant amount of tickets he teased her with. And then it was Laura's turn. After that, Hellen. Faith. Lydia…

Returning to her rooms wasn't hard. Eugenia's daily schedule robotic, hour to hour, the same. Day in and day out. Breaks for menstruation. All free time spent reading *Nelson's Textbook of Pediatrics*—pages she had all but memorized.

No point in counting the weeks, the show of a guard after the buzz from 'the captain fucking her' died down. She was no longer considered fresh. His hypothetical cock some form of magic. The men stopped coming on so strong. Their belief that the captain had plowed that field taking a bit of shine off the apple.

Especially because there was a new girl far more enthusiastic about her life of luxury on the ship. So happy, in fact, she could not stop going on about how great it was.

Air conditioning, regular meals, clean sheets, a real mattress, pretty things...

And some of the other women were beginning to agree with the feel-good positivity.

Even agreeing that they enjoyed the attention of eager men who'd spruced up and saved just to see them.

As for prompted sex? The pretty, new brunette came when they mounted her from behind at the tables. Porn-star loud.

The captain commended her and upgraded Juanita to the best room a girl could have. She was an example to live by. And an enigma Eugenia could not wrap her thoughts around.

She didn't like her. Everyone else did though, because Juanita was sweet, bubbly, playful, and genuinely nice.

Eugenia didn't like her, because Juanita was simple.

*Because the newcomer was happy.*

And it was starting to settle in that no matter what, Eugenia was never going to be. Maybe never had been.

So the escape attempts she'd been calculating for months began to unfold. The first was simple, find the stairwells and just walk off the boat.

That led to another kicking and screaming ride on another male shoulder only to be dumped at the scowling captain's boots.

Next option? Climb down railings where life rafts used to be. Torn bed sheets, cursing, and sorry loss of upper arm strength led her to be caught only three floors down.

So she took to standing at the railing of Level 15, looking down and calculating the physics.

No one would survive that fall.

Well, they might survive the fall… but they would not survive the damage done to their body upon breaking the lapping water's meniscus.

"Look, Miss. I really have better things to do than follow you around all day and make sure you don't kill yourself."

"For fuck's sake, Stewart! Do I look like I'm prepping to kill myself? How the fuck would I live a life off this boat if I'm dead?" Red curls flying, she abandoned the math to stare down her babysitter. "I don't have to play nice with you until dinner. And I'm only going to do it then, because your jokes are decent and you are legitimately skilled at chess. Meanwhile. Be quiet."

Sincere, gentle, that prick said, "You're not getting off the boat."

"Shut up. Of course I am."

So earnest it made the fine hairs on her neck stand, he asked, "But why? Don't you like the life we give you?"

"Give me twenty-million tickets and I'll explain it in grand detail."

There was no reason for a random man to look at her that way. "We all like you. You like us, right?"

Blinking, Eugenia cocked her head. New math forming in her head. He was a strapping man, young enough to be useful. Gay as the day was long. "I could show you how to live. Hunt for us. Teach you what to look for. Why not come with me?"

"That's it. I'm done here." And Stewart was done. "I don't care if I get in trouble. You're nuts, and I'm not gonna stand here and watch you be nuts anymore."

"I'll see you at dinner, handsome!" she shouted at his back.

And she did. But it was an uncomfortable feast—Juanita was sobbing hysterically as she learned just how horrible her new heaven was.

And every guest, every server, every *girl* scheduled to entertain knew why.

Pretty Juanita had mentioned one particular man too many times. Was extra excited to see him. *She'd fallen in love.*

And so had the man Juanita favored.

But unlike Neil, he had known better than to offer for her.

Instead, he slapped her, hard, in front of them all at a party. The big man crying and sputtering the whole time he called her a whore.

It wasn't a secret that Eugenia and the captain traded words every day—a few minutes here and few minutes there—but it was the first time besides the night he ripped her hymen on dirty fingers that she'd approached him.

The captain…

…who was watching her and not the tableau on deck. Who had been watching her the whole time.

"Aaron," she offered.

A tip of the chin. "Eugenia."

Arms around her middle, the day having been a shit waste of her time. Feeling naked under his stare for a reason she could not pin, she said, "I think you should let them be together."

"Why? Why should they get what the rest of the ship can't have?"

How could he sound so reasonable when two people were in so much pain?

Hard to think, even harder to say, Eugenia bared her thoughts. "Because they love each other. The real kind."

Hazel eyes bearing down upon her as if she were the only person on that entire crowded deck, the captain said, "They've known one another a handful of weeks. Love? That ain't the real kind. Nor would it last as she kept playing around, which she would, because she likes the attention, the favors, the upgrades, and cock."

How he could continue to reduce them all to comfort sluts, she couldn't grasp. Why couldn't *forever* be real in a place that was so bad? "What if you're wrong? What if that love at first sight bullshit is true?"

Throat bobbing, he swallowed before he might speak.

Not that she refused to give him the stage to wax poetic on his crazy rules. Not when someone might actually find joy in all this shit. "Can I take her inside?" The request was followed with a quick, "I'll come right back, work both tables, and be the dumpster in trade. Give Faith and Chloe a night off. Give Juanita a chance to… think."

Raising a knee, he let his boot rest against the wall at his back. "But you don't even like her."

Which didn't matter at all. "I don't like anyone. I'm antisocial and a pretentious jerk; you know that."

Laughing, a bitter, hard sound, he laid out the cost. "You'll owe me a favor."

"And you owe me so much more than that." Which led to a stirring of dark feelings swallowed way, way down. "*You owe me so much more, Aaron.*"

The cocky bastard smirked. "That lip is going to cost you another ten-thousand tickets."

"Fuck your tickets! I don't need them. And yes, you'll have your favor, though I suggest you don't abuse it."

"You know I will, darlin'." The lazy cowboy act, the accent. All of it a show as he brushed her cheek with his knuckles.

In a way, it was hard to admit she knew him on a level the others didn't. "I'm going to take Juanita inside."

"If you need to talk it over, I'm here."

"Suck the fattest cock, Aaron."

Sobbing, crying into her shoulder the whole way, a *girl*—a brokenhearted *girl* who'd been struck by a brokenhearted boy—wept out her grief.

And there was nothing to be done for it but share the ship's ugly truth.

Eugenia told her about Neil. Whispered that if she wanted to enjoy her lover, Juanita had to keep it secret like the other girls did. That she'd never have more than a quick kiss and tryst in the hall. That she had to be careful to show him little favor in public.

That the captain could never know—and if he found out, her lover was a dead man.

So buck up! Earn tickets with enthusiasm, buy her freedom. Maybe he could buy his; they could leave together. Wouldn't that be great?

Which, even as Eugenia said it, she knew it would never happen. The game was rigged, and Juanita was too good a treasure to lose. A whore enthusiastic to be fucked, and not just to earn tickets. She loved sex when it wasn't forced. And who could blame her?

Which led to the thorn ridden path of self-awareness—the real reason Eugenia didn't like the exuberant new girl. She was jealous.

Of the participation. Of the orgasms. Of any shred of fun others might enjoy when there was nothing but work and service and the never-ending foiled attempts to escape.

Eugenia couldn't let go or live up.

How clever the captain had been, stroking her when she'd been in his rooms. Growling at her ear that he cared. Urging her to explore her body in private and remember how wonderful masturbation had felt.

The release, relearning her body.

Her own fingers slipping through sensitive labia, twisting over a hooded clit. Until it poked out and she tapped it just like she used to.

How beautiful it was to come.

Every night. In private.

To fantasies dug up from memory. To Li Wei's sexy body, to his voice, which had grown deeper, his weight more pronounced when it pushed her down in that sleeping bag.

Eugenia touched herself. Fantasized about freedom, equality, a man who loved her. A man near her intelligence level who accepted she was smarter. A doctor…

She fantasized.

Ached for the kind of fulfilment she'd never find the way sweet Juanita had, bent over a table and plowed by the line of eager men for tickets.

Sweet Juanita who was looking at her with beautiful, wet, wide brown eyes. Who needed the comfort of a wiser, older person.

Eugenia had not felt like a person in quite some time.

"The captain is giving you the night off. Have a shower and a good cry. Sleep." That was the best advice she might offer, leaving an apartment almost as nice as the captain's to get back to the party.

Pausing outside the door that separated the women's rooms from the party deck, she found the captain waiting for her.

So she confessed, "I learned something about myself tonight."

Passing a toothpick from one side of his mouth to the other, he asked, "Care to share your newfound wisdom?"

Detached, she told the captain, "No."

A thing like him wouldn't understand.

A thing like him should not have reached for her arm and pulled her back. "You did a good thing tonight, Eugenia. I'm proud."

But anger was the first and only thing she knew. "He hit her because you made him do it."

"And?"

And what? "I have work to do. Enjoy your nightly show, slaver. Fuck a trafficked person later, tying them up so they don't look at you while you do it. I hope you hate every moment of it as much as I think you do."

# Chapter Ten

White-knuckling the railing, far above the faded, red nonslip carpet gracing the gangplank, Eugenia strained against the heat of the captain at her back. Saw the way his hands banked hers, and screamed.

Nothing could be worse!

*The favor*—a few minutes of her time, he'd said.

Where no one could see the pair of them together. Where their view was unobstructed. Where he pinned her mercilessly. Where she was engulfed in a larger, stronger body. Not out of intimacy, but to keep her from running away. Or jumping to her death when she began to panic.

Because the ship's lights were on.

And though it was a long, *long* way down, a familiar voice carried up. "Please! I beg you! Please let me back in!"

Even from the distance, it was clear who it was.

Brooke—emaciated, limping, and covered in filthy rags—staggered toward the lake, waving her arms. Beseeching the waiting men for help.

Wretched. Broken. Sick.

With their guns on their backs, the men were at the ready. Prepping a dinghy to fetch the pleading woman before she might accidentally drown in her fervor to stamp through the lake and get back on the ship.

"NO!" Eugenia screamed.

*And screamed.*

What was this life but endurance past pain?

But the captain had clamped his hand over her mouth, her muffled warning lost no matter how hard she fought.

And she fought with all she had. Kicking, throwing elbows, biting at his palm to warn the girl away. That it was a trick. That real life was *out there*.

Why would she come back to this?

She should RUN!

But his arm, like iron around her waist, was so much bigger and stronger.

He caught her strikes, took her wrists in hand, as if he'd done it thousands of times.

Just like he had with the other women tied to his bed so he might fuck them from behind and they might sleep on his couch.

Brooke was fetched. She was carried on board.

The show was over.

Subdued by muscle, mouth freed, hate roaring, tears flowed in an excruciating, embarrassing way. "Why would she come back? At least one good place is out there! All the bad places had been marked on that map! She has to explain!"

Though his grip was unbreakable, his voice was infinitely soft. "Brooke won't be coming back to Level 15."

"I... I don't understand." Could hardly even breathe. Couldn't look at him. Only at those boots. At the deck and her splayed fingers, white as death, scratching as if they might find something to hold.

A kiss lingered on her temple before he said, "You won't like it. You won't like why Level 9 exists. Which is precisely why you've never asked about babies or children. Because you are so close to growing up, and so scared to face it. You've blinded yourself to the obvious."

"Stop talking!"

"Neil told you that first day. *The men don't get to hold the babies,* but they do get to breed them, provide for them. Know that there is a future. A future the men know they will never have. The best they can do is make the women comfortable, feed them good food."

Hands over her ears, pressing as hard as she could, Eugenia failed to keep his words out.

"It's a big ship, Eugenia. An entire society of people that function with minimal violence and maximum growth. The perfect equation, a tight rein on circular history.

"Brooke will earn her keep as a breeder, *as a mother*, finding her peace with it like they all do. As will Hellen, Juanita, Chloe..."

She was going to be sick, right there on his boots, yet raised her eyes to look at the monster, to read him like she could. "How many women have you done this to?"

"Only the pretty ones of a certain age experience Level 15 and the workload involved. Everyone else is hosted on Level 9. Twenty-four women counting Brooke."

It didn't seem possible that she could have thought worse of this place, of him. But it was so much worse than she'd imagined. "Can they buy their way out?"

"No. I can't have them taking babies off the boat." Holding her eyes as if his gaze alone might pin her in place, as if it might change her thinking, he gestured to the dead forest and the dirty lake.

"Children don't belong out there. No one knows that better than you. Brooke will be given time to adjust and heal. She may already be pregnant, which will buy her more time to settle in with her baby before she will be expected to do her part and submit to the man who purchased rights to her cycle. All copulation is monitored, genealogies tracked, and the men know they have to try to please their lady for the month. *Foreplay is required.* It costs them a fortune, and there is a waiting list a mile long. Level 15 is what tides them over while they wait to play house."

Foreplay? He was the king of foreplay, and she was the queen of surviving bullshit. "How many of the kids are yours?"

"None." He shook his head. "I don't go to Level 9."

"Why? Can't look them in the eye when you can't even fuck Level 15 slaves face-to-face?"

"Work out the statistics, work your math, and admit to yourself that I'm trying to save the world." He had not been that harsh with her since the day his fingers tore her hymen. But he was sharp as a razor as he condemned, "I know you don't want to face the truth, because you're too damn bitter over what you lost. *Everyone lost,* Eugenia! And everyone had a part in it. And now everyone pays."

Not on this boat. "Except you, in your fancy room with your music and rotating harem of pretty girls of a certain age. You're a monster, Aaron." Slinking out from his touch, she skittered back. "I don't ever want to talk to you again. I don't even want to look at you."

Standing tall, he sighed. As if he was the one hurting and she was the one causing it. "You'll come to accept it. They all do."

He walked away, leaving her as she was—because they both knew she wasn't going to throw herself over that railing—Eugenia screaming at his back, "When I get off this boat, I won't ever come back!"

***

Ironically forced to dress in the same outfit from that first, awful night—the naughty schoolgirl—Eugenia prepared Table #2. Stacking the pile of linen to the side for the men to shoot their load into. Grasping why they never complained about not finishing in the *girls*.

Because it would break their fancy toy if that human got pregnant. After all, everyone went to Level 9, and they'd have their shot later.

And they all knew it when they teased, kissed, adored, fucked, and offered for Level 15 girls.

They weren't straight evil. The captain was. And she could see how some of them had hinted. But who could doubt for a minute that outright spilling the beans about Level 9 led to instant execution?

Couldn't upset this well-oiled machine of mind games and carnival tickets, now could they?

Fuck up the party if the party girls realized the ride never ended.

So, what was down there? Women chained to beds? Is that why he liked to tie the other girls up? Get them accustomed to it.

What did the men trade for the opportunity to breed an entire cycle?

Five-thousand tickets? Five-hundred thousand?

Whatever Brooke had just survived might make that woman go mad if a man tried to touch her. Maybe the captain's version of acceptance was just a bunch of broken shells with functioning wombs and severe psychological trauma.

Brooke was in bad shape.

She limped like the dying limped.

But stranded on Level 15, Eugenia couldn't help her. Spending her hour analyzing a gait she'd seen only once from hundreds of feet away.

Remembering that scream for help.

Knowing she was being mocked all the time by the captain. The only person on that whole fucking ship who had been her "friend."

God, she was an idiot.

The things she had told Aaron in their daily banter.

The ways he would have to suffer before he died.

Did the men all laugh at her below deck? The fallen virgin who thought she was so damn smart? Who they all knew would end up as some kind of breeder on Level 9 no matter how long she held out.

Who they indulged.

Men she knew. Who she'd conversed with for months. Men who sat at her table that very night as she brushed lint from the white tablecloth. Men who presented their cookie sheets for her to sit on. Who bantered and dined on ribeye, *just like that first night.*

There hadn't been ribeye since…

Not that it mattered. Twenty-million-plus tickets she owed. Ten fucks a night, she might get off the ship in two years. Walk south and never stop walking. Never stop.

Ever.

The man with his hand splayed on her belly, who served as her chair, said, "You're awfully quiet tonight. Are you okay?"

On no level was she okay. "I'm just doing some math… a bit stuck on the numbers."

How many plates had she broken? How many extra fucks had she added to her tally?

If she could convince ten of them to fuck her a night, how many nights would that be? There were only five men at her table, so she'd have to draw the other men, get competitive over tickets. Would ten men even want to fuck her every day, or would she look as worn out as Chloe? Who was no doubt going to be transitioned to Level 9… because she'd almost earned enough by whoring the hardest.

That was why Chloe had put glass shards in Juanita's food her first night. Fresh and pretty competition extended this hell. And that's why Juanita was warned about the glass, just like Eugenia had been—Captain's orders, no doubt.

That's what affected their price. How much ride the captain thought he could get out of all of them.

"You look pale, Eugenia."

The things she had confided in these men. Her history. Her achievements and blunders. Funny childhood stories and the names of her dead parents. Despite never intending to, she had connected with them on an extremely fucked-up level.

And they were all in on it.

She meant to answer with something canned. A general "I'm fine." But her eyes finally lifted from that tablecloth… and it wasn't her guests she saw.

It was John.

Perched at Table #6. Having fun as he lined up for a turn. He laughed, though didn't engage in the banter.

He didn't have a tongue. The captain had told her so.

She wasn't sure how she got there, or why she thought a goddamn cookie sheet would serve to kill him. The drag on each swing—thanks to the shape of her chosen weapon—slowed down momentum and reduced impact.

Not that it mattered when sanity had fled. Beating him with all she had, she screamed that she'd kill him for doing this to her. Turning the cookie sheet to its side when it clicked that it would be far more effective to reduce wind resistance.

Going straight for the throat.

Six months!

She'd been on the ship at least six months for him to have earned his way up to Level 15.

When his fist landed in her gut, when he took her down like a linebacker to steal the rest of her air, she refused to let him steal the rest of her life.

Rage fortified. Claws going for the eyes.

Men tried to pull them apart. There was a great deal of shouting when she tore an eyelid.

When she bit back.

"I'll fucking kill you, John! You're a dead man!" It took at least three burly men to tear her from her prey. "Don't think you can hide behind the boys. I'll find you, you coward! I SAVED YOUR LIFE AND YOU SOLD ME TO MONSTERS!"

One of many who had grappled her to the floor lost a grip and earned a broken nose for it. "Christ, she's strong, Captain!"

But she didn't care. Her attention was laser-focused on a *boy* held back, who was also bleeding, but who was not fighting for freedom. Because he felt safe being male, and she was just a dumb whore.

"You'll die, John. I'll see it through!"

Her line of sight was spoiled by an all too familiar face, a person who dared say, “Don’t look at him. Look at me. Hear what I’m saying to you, Eugenia. If you don’t calm down, I’m going to have to calm you down. And I’m asking you not to make me do that.”

Fuck all of it! “Aaron, I can’t do this anymore.” Tears, desperation. All the things she’d kept in. “I can’t.”

Gaze so heavy she’d rather carry a thousand tons, he murmured, “Take a deep breath for me.”

She did, one that shook all the way into her aching ribs. And then another one. And another. Until she stopped fighting and the men cautiously let her go.

Not that she hesitated to slap off their arms as if it made any difference.

Looking down at herself. At her stupid outfit and the way her tits were held back with nothing but a couple buttons. The front of a silly shirt tied under her bosom, midriff on display.

Li Wei would have hated that outfit. His conservative mother would have had a heart attack at first glance. Neither of them would have ever hit her.

And they were dead.

And it was over.

Undoing that first button was remarkably easy. The second one, nothing at all. After all, it was a question of math. Could be reduced to statistics. A desperation worse than any mental lapse to escape that horrible place.

Her third button popped, the captain squinting as he demanded to know, "What are you doing?"

Giving in. Giving in as she flipped up the pleated skirt and let the men see lace panties. "Who wants to go first?"

Not one of them moved to take her, wide, wet eyes begging, no matter how they gawked. "Come now, red light special at Table #2. I'll go for as long as I can take it. Five-thousand tickets a ride."

And still, no one touched her. After all their offers—after all their rejected presents and dirty talk over chess—not one of them made a move.

So she did. Standing, the captain mirrored her movement.

Which suited just fine.

His tickets were as good as any other man there. Hand to his buckle, she fought off his restraint. "Face-to-face the first time? Isn't that how it goes? Ass in the air after?"

Oh, was he mad. Mad enough to give her a shake. "That's enough out of you."

"I'm not joking!" Red curls went flying as she fought to pull his shirt from his pants. "I want off this goddamn boat, and if that means I have to fuck everyone on it to get there, then I'm ready."

The clown of the show started laughing, John's amusement meaner than any slight she'd heard in her entire life.

The sound off, because he was missing a tongue for telling tales.

Not that it mattered.

Not really.

The only thing that mattered she couldn't reach, despite his ugly guffaws. "I'll even fuck John."

The captain's command was given lightly. "Throw him overboard."

Order followed before John might comprehend why, those nearest him hoisted him up and sent him cartwheeling through freefall.

He screamed all the way down. And must have landed feet first, bones shattered, to yell as his broken body tried to swim and sank.

A good minute, he thrashed for life, not a soul at the party making a sound.

One soul swallowing it down as if a kiss had touched her lips for the first time in years.

Opening her eyes, infinitesimally lighter in spirit, she met the captain's hazel gaze and said, "I thought foreplay was against the rules."

# Chapter Eleven

Aaron didn't find her quip funny. Looked angrier than she'd ever seen him. "Go to my room. Clean yourself up. I want you naked on the bed when I get there."

It wasn't so bad a plan. She'd start with the captain and get him out of the way. More importantly, the rest of the men might be more eager if she wasn't bloody and wild-looking. Brushing her hands on her mussed skirt as if smoothing the Chanel suit she'd worn for her Harvard Med scholarship interview, she pulled herself together in a way that would have made her mother proud.

And walked away without a word.

Operating on instinct, allowing no thought, she washed herself, felt no pain as grit was scrubbed from abrasion. Raided the pirate king's medicine cabinet for precious aspirin and bandages. He'd charge her for them, but she needed to be a presentable fuck.

Because her new goal was nothing but tickets, tickets, and more tickets.

Wet curls combed, her pussy shaved for the first time in her life, she sat at the edge of his bed and stared forward. There was no acknowledgement when the door opened, no acknowledgment of the man who had come to take what she sold.

Kneeling down in front of her, he held ice to her cheek, hushing her when she startled.

"I don't need that."

"I say you do, troublemaker." Another hand to her knee, he gave it an easy squeeze. "It's going to swell up something awful if you don't hold still."

A little spite, a lot of bitterness. "Are you going to order me to call you Doctor while we do it?"

"I technically am a doctor, so you wouldn't be the first."

She rolled her eyes, which didn't help the headache.

With a chuckle, he explained, "Multiple PHDs, former professor at Tulane. I taught history and philosophy."

"You have got to be kidding me…"

Smirking, he confirmed, "Dr. Aaron Kingston."

Jealous down to her toes that he'd made it academically further than she had, Eugenia sneered. "And here I thought you were some kind of renegade cowboy soldier."

"Former Navy. Family tradition. My grandfather was the governor of Mississippi. Also a family tradition."

"What a fancy pedigree… one which explains a lot. Mississippi had a terrible track record for human rights." As much as he was right about the ice, she didn't have time to waste. "Let's stop with the small talk. I have a bunch of tickets to make. And it isn't my night to be in here, so I want Hellen's tickets too. Unless you can go more than once…"

Voice husky, he made a promise. "We're going to go more than once."

"All right then." And she scooted back to get on her hands and knees.

Or, *tried* to scoot back and was caught. Tired of the endless struggles, she put up a token effort before flopping still and laying an arm over her eyes. "I don't want to do it face-to-face like this matters. I know what you said about first times, but you have a pass. Can we please just get it over with?"

"Look at me, Eugenia."

Obeying the order, she found him standing between her legs, unbuttoning his shirt while he held her eyes. While he took his measured time removing one item of clothing after another, exposing brawn, defined abs, a body that would have graced GQ pre-bombs.

Hair on his chest, strong laborer's body, southern aristocracy. Cocky, because he was born to it. And he did have an unusually large penis.

One that, frankly, made her a bit nervous.

A hard cock that pulsed with the beats of his heart as it grew even larger. Foreskin drawn back, that delectable ridge running along the bottom.

"No one is going to want to fuck me after that rips me in half." And it *was* going to hurt. And there was a mental quota that didn't have time for recovery nights. "Hellen can keep her tickets."

He laughed when she tried and failed, again, to crawl away. "I know it's a bit daunting, but considering your medical training, I'm fairly certain you grasp that the vaginal canal was designed to stretch."

"For babies, not for massive, freakish cocks!"

It didn't look like he intended to argue anymore, creeping over her to plant a kiss right on her mouth.

“Aaron! Kissing is not allowed!”

Not that her swallowed complaints stopped him from dipping his tongue into her open mouth. Just like the secret lovers who kissed in dark halls on a boat where rules lead to misery and misery led to survival. Languid and keen, he drank her down no matter her lack of reciprocation. Nipping her bottom lip before kissing her jaw.

Holding her still by the roots of her red hair.

Getting his money’s worth as he took every last taste.

“Kiss me, Eugenia.”

If it would end this sooner, then fine. She kissed him.

And he groaned, settling further against her body, and began to nudge his knee so she might spread hers. Which was the point, right?

So she threw her all into that kiss, taking in equal parts to what he gave. Letting his tongue play over hers, allowing the invasion as his chest hair tickled her nipples.

Always the mind reader, he abandoned her mouth to suck a pink tip into his mouth. A bit too hard—absolutely perfect. Nipping and sucking and all tongue. One, then the other. Kneading heavy breasts, pressing and pulling flesh in a way that stole her senses.

Then that wicked mouth traveled down her stomach. Until he was kneeling between her legs and she was spread wide before him. Gripping her hips, he pulled her straight to his mouth.

And she got to experience *the tongue thing*. And, Jesus, it really was something worth bragging over.

Sore fingers fisting his covers, dying inside because it felt so good, Eugenia locked her thighs around his face and took.

When he entered her with two fingers, she tensed, then survived a full-body shudder when he curled them upward and found a place inside her no other ever had. Growing rougher with that come-hither motion, what should have hurt was the exact opposite. She didn't even need that masterful tongue on her clit.

She came, drenching his hand, and fairly certain she was an inch away from the afterlife.

It went on and on as he did things no southern gentleman should. A pirate until she begged him to stop and he still refused.

Orgasms shouldn't last so long. And no lady should saturate the coverlet while a pirate ate her alive.

In a daze, she caught the way he let a string of spit leave his mouth to coat the overlarge cock he worked in his hand. Registered that he had crept over her body to position himself to take what she had preserved—the only symbol of who she had been before bombs fell and the world grew poisoned.

The last piece of her.

A simple hole where the first penis *ever* was slowly pushing forward, breaching a place that should not have mattered anymore.

But did. She felt the loss of so much when pain snapped her out of despair.

A burning sting washing away unattainable history, dragging her mentally kicking to the present.

"Relax." How softly he said it for a man that was so hard. "There you go. A little more. You *can* take me. I promise."

This man and his promises, and his rules, and his unwavering self.

A man who was right far more often than he should be—who had claimed there would be blood. There would be, whatever remained of her already torn hymen annihilated.

Breathing too hard and too fast. Tense, embarrassingly nervous, legs shaking, and unbearably full of someone else, Eugenia held his eyes as he talked her through her first time.

Held them when he began to rock his hips. To fuck her.

Held them when it started to feel good despite the sting. His body working over hers, his lips singing praises. Hands keeping hers pinned by her head, so there didn't need to be a struggle.

And she held them when, for some inexplicable reason, her vagina began to pulsate. When she joined his rhythm.

Climaxing all over the first cock that had ever been inside her—thrown by the force of it—she turned her head and bit his wrist until he bled just as she did.

Until her muffled scream came to an end, and she floated in between a placated body and a disconnected mind. Too stupid and inexperienced to grasp what followed upon his growl.

It wasn't until he pulled out and a trickle escaped to drip over her anus that it registered.

He came inside her!

And because math is where she hid when everything needed to be sorted, counting the days, Eugenia knew it wasn't safe. Tried to remember the probability of conceiving during ovulation, even as he laid kisses on every inch of her flesh he might plunder.

"It's a six-percent chance, right? No, at my age, that can't be right. Is it ten? Fuck, is it thirty?" Struggling under him, unsure why he wasn't moving, considering this was the rule that was never broken, she shoved and shoved at a strong male body that would not be moved. "Do I wash it out?"

But there was no washing it out, not pinned as she was. Not when the captain was not in a talking mood no matter her panicked questions or attempts to reach down and remove what was turning from cream into a watery mess. Not when he refused to speak with her unless it was to lick at her breasts and tell her how delicious they were. Complimenting every last inch. Describing in detail how she'd felt around his cock.

Seeking out the secret places on her body that distracted and hardened her clit—that unlike past lovers he had no problem finding to tease.

He fucked her again and again. Made her come.

Ejaculated inside her with *intention*.

Until the sun came up and she begged for rest.

One of the most traumatic days of her life, followed by an inexplicable night that marked her as something she'd yet to come to terms with, too tired to fight back.

Someone sore and desperate for sleep. "Sleep deprivation is a form of torture, you know. I can't keep up with you."

On so many very fucked-up levels, she could not keep up with him in most ways.

"Rest, love." There was another, sensual, deadly kiss before he turned her into his body, hooking his leg over her hip. His arm her pillow, the other one her prison.

# Chapter Twelve

It wasn't the sound of the shower that woke her. It was the door.

Joan bearing burlap bags of God only knew what. Joan with a friendly nod as if she had walked in on the familiar scene of another naked woman sitting up on the captain's bed. Because this was commonplace, and Eugenia was no different than the rest of them.

The same women Eugenia had silently judged. The same women who had been far more savvy and now ultimately ten steps ahead of her. Who'd earn their freedom long before the uptight redhead did—the idiot redhead and her goddamn, unimportant virginity.

"Joan, I need your help." It didn't matter that she was naked, bruised thighs, lovebites, fingermarks, and other signs of exactly what happened on full display. It didn't matter that Eugenia was frantic now that some sleep had returned her sense of reason. Only one thing mattered.

"Are you sore? I prepared an ice pack that should help with the swelling. It's wrapped in soft towels you can rest right between your legs. And don't forget to drink a lot of water and urinate often."

How kindly sage advice was administered. How naturally, because this was a common event and the man truly did have a horse cock.

"No. Listen." She took the old woman by the shoulders, knowing her kiss-swollen lips shook as she pleaded. "He came inside me. I didn't know to stop him. The morning after pill? Is there some trick the women use? What do I do? Joan, help me!"

Gentle hands urged her back to the bed, to spread quivering thighs for an extremely personal view. "Let's take a look, okay? Up with you, girl."

*Woman.*

Though women probably didn't freak out over spilled semen in such epic proportions.

"Let me guess." Eugenia winced when ungloved fingers slipped inside her to poke around. "You're a gynecologist."

"Midwife." Said with such pride. "There, I feel it... your cervix is soft. You're fertile. Now you wait. Should it take, you and Brooke will deliver a couple months apart."

Brooke? She'd been back a day and it was already confirmed she was pregnant? And of course the old hag was in on the whole fucked-up enslavement of her own sex!

"You're so goddamn lucky you've gone through menopause." Shoving Joan away, pulling bedding over her body because this could not stand, Eugenia went from desperate to furious. "Enough with the madame act. How do the other girls keep a baby out? There has to be some post-apocalyptic trick, right? Some chant? Poison tea?" Woman-to-woman, she called her out for Joan's part in all the ugliness. "For the love of God, don't let him do this to me! I will not go to Level 9."

A watery drip of what had been left inside her leaked out. Anger morphing back to horror as she looked down as if she might see old semen run its course despite the blanket covering her nakedness. "It's still coming out."

Smelling like the enemy, having memorized exactly how he tasted, Eugenia shivered, clutching the bedding closer as if it might shield her. "How could I be so stupid? He planned all of it. John's attendance at dinner the same night Brooke returned. Did they keep her roaming the woods until my cycle entered a fertility window? Did the men hide packs on corpses with food and water for Brooke? Leaving a trail to the pretty ship's lights, struck up to welcome her home… so I might see and be manipulated into giving him exactly what he wanted?"

Hands before her, Joan shook her head. "You are an extremely intelligent young lady, which is why we both know what you're saying is crazy."

No, it wasn't. The captain *was* that smart.

Confirmed when a roguish viper wearing nothing but a towel spoke from where he watched his script play out. “But accurate.” Glancing to the older woman, he said, “Joan, thank you for bringing her things. Please lock the door behind you.”

Which the woman did immediately, an ominous click following her exit.

There had to be a way to outthink this, some strategy on the chessboard before the timer clicked and Eugenia lost her chance to take the king. Yet… the feeling of betrayal?

Hurt.

She had trusted Aaron in a really fucked-up way.

“Good morning, Eugenia.” How normal a greeting. One he had offered her since their first meeting on the ship. Polite, with that cowboy swagger and smirk.

“This is…” Blinking like mad, calculations running wild in her overtaxed brain, looking anywhere but at him, she held up a hand. "I just need a moment to think."

Yet he sauntered closer, the towel dangling dangerously from his hips. "You don't have to love me back. But you do need to understand that I will never let you off this ship. I can't. The world doesn't deserve you."

How funny, she could still laugh despite all of it. Though it came out choked in an embarrassingly high pitch. "And you do?"

Knee to the bed, he proceeded to edge all the nearer. "I gave you six months to come to terms with what we both know I wanted. Six months in which you maintained chastity until you told me, dead on, you were ready."

Twisting the situation much? "That is not what I meant and you know it!"

"Yell at me, brandish those claws, but hear this. Before witnesses, you accepted me. Obeyed when ordered to go to my rooms, to wash up, to wait for me naked."

What the fuck did any of that matter? She'd done it for the tickets. "And?"

"You went." Spoken softly, simply, as if he was trying to lead her to some preconceived outcome. As if everyone else knew something she didn't.

"Jesus, Aaron! Just stop! This is not a fucking game of chess." One hand holding the sheet, the other tearing at her curls, she felt embarrassingly overwrought. "You screwed me for tickets! I let you do whatever you wanted, did whatever you asked. Tickets you now owe me. And I will get more—from every last piece of shit you have working on your boat until I have paid your imaginary debt. I will deepthroat like the fucking champion I am! And when I get off, unlike Brooke, I won't ever come back."

Drinking her in, the captain took a deep, rib-expanding breath. "We never negotiated a price; therefore… I owe you nothing. Also witnessed." With a hard look, he added, "Don't give me that wide-eyed fury. You've been here long enough to know how the game works."

"You cheated! Which, in the effort of full disclosure, is gutting, Aaron. Well done." But there wasn't time to worry over that. Besides, what was one lost night? Virginity aside, she'd get over it, because there was a whole life that still needed to be lived. "You're not the first opponent who couldn't win fair and square, and now I'll make it damn clear before any services are exchanged exactly how much I cost. Maybe I should thank you for telling me before another of them tried what you pulled. I don't have the time to waste."

Calm despite her temper, he shook his head. "Not one of them will touch you."

She too could be cocky, flipping her sex-mussed curls over her shoulder. "Of course they will! I'm propositioned for sex more often than I'm offered a hello."

As she'd been born annoyingly attractive, men had always embarrassed themselves—either over her hair, her tits, or her face.

A curse when trying to be taken seriously in academia. A boon in competition of any kind against the straight opposite sex.

Until now.

"Don't get me wrong, siren. Every last one of them would like to. But they can't." The captain looked so damn pleased with himself. Railing his fingers down his overly defined abs as if to entice her to see all he had on offer. As if to remind her how good he'd been the night before. "You belong to me."

Which deserved peels of unhinged laughter. "You got twenty-something-million tickets sitting on a roll you've tucked away for just such an occasion? I mean, if you're telling me you paid the price, I can walk right off this boat."

His grin grew. "Well, the door is locked, so you're going to have a hard time with that."

"You leave me locked in this room and I will bust apart your wood furnishings and use the fragments to start a fire. A spindle, determination, friction... I've done it before. And my hands have the calluses to prove it."

He shook his head, countering, "There are children and babies on this boat. More than you'd expect. We take them all in, seek them out, and, *as you know*, create more."

Deep inhale, closed eyes, pursed lips exhale. Her lashes flared open, heartrate leveling. "I'll give you this. I don't think you've ever outright lied to me. That's not your trick. So get to the point. Describe, in detail, what you intend to do now."

"This is the question you should have asked six months ago. But you clung to safety in an ideal—one we both knew was ludicrous—because it was the only thing you had left." Close enough to touch her now, her sheet, his towel, all that was between them beside a mountain of female regret. "You're stubborn, you're smart, and you use anger like a shield, because without it, you'd fall to pieces."

Oh, he wanted to dig in the knife, while she knew a thing or two about him. "And you fuck the women as many nights as you can tolerate it, *because they degraded themselves to earn tickets*, and the burden of the chore should be shared. You're the real whore on this ship. You fucked them, you fucked me, for pay."

"You're not entirely wrong."

"Does it make you feel better to play your part in the show? Those blowjobs where the women try to get you to look them in the eye, where they show off to earn favor? Is it different for men? Is an orgasm just an orgasm?"

"We made love last night. It was different."

"I DID IT FOR TICKETS!"

"No, you didn't. You did it, because I'd taken your last excuse away and you were starved."

"And you came in me." The hurt in her voice, knowing her eyes stung and that he could see it… was killing her. "You came in me, Aaron. That was wrong."

Cupping her cheek, he used his thumb to wipe the single spilt tear. "Eugenia, honey, I waited six months. You can't blame me for being unable to wait any longer. I know what I did. I know what I'm going to do. Because I'm starved too."

"It all sounds so pretty when you say it that way, but I remember clearly what you said yesterday. You don't go down to Level 9."

"I'll make an exception."

More tears came. "Is it begging that you want from me? You can have it. You already took everything else. Please don't put me down there. Give me the same chance you give the rest of the women. Let me earn my way off."

Pain in his voice, he said, "You think I'd be able to survive watching that?"

"And why should you get to have what no one else on this ship is allowed?" A fair question, but spoken with rancor.

Trailing his touch from her face, down her throat, soft over the tops of her breasts, the captain hooked a finger where his sheet covered her, pulling enough to warn that she best let go. "You know why."

But she held that sheet. That final, wispy barrier between them. Held tight. "I'm not pregnant."

Cocky smile, the male looked right at her kiss-swollen mouth. "We can work on that."

With a flourish, the blanket was ripped away, thrown to the floor, despite Eugenia's yelp and sorry attempt to catch it.

Hot lips landed on her shoulder, the captain pressing her down to the bedding, pulling at the towel around his hips and fighting his way between her thighs. As if she were wet and ready.

Which she was not.

His belligerent, deliberate penetration with that massive, uncut dick burned. Burned enough that, despite her proactive enthusiasm the night before, she hissed in pain. "It hurts!"

And he too looked pained, as if pressing in so slow, even as she fought to force him out, tore him apart. "I know you're sore on multiple levels. And you know I'm substantial. Which is why, when this is done, I'll make it better."

“Aaron, please.” Spreading her legs because it hurt a whole lot less, screwing her eyes shut, because no man should look at a woman that way, she whimpered, “You were my only friend.”

And that was so totally fucked up she didn’t even know how to continue.

Like a preacher at his pulpit, he gave his sermon, invaded deeper still. “More than your friend, Eugenia. Now, tell me you feel me inside you.”

It was hard to say, hard to breathe. “Yes.”

“And I’m going to stay there. I won’t share you with the others. It’s my babies you’ll carry. And like I said, you don't have to love me back, but you do have to stay.”

He was too much, the intrusion so much more than cock in vaginal canal. It was how he’d worked his way into her routines, her mind… a familiar tear through the walls she’d built. And it was too much to be borne.

Balls-deep, firmly planted, he whispered, “I do love you.”

And she sobbed all the harder.

"I'll even get you a ring if you want one."

She shook her head, eyes screwed shut and aching all over.

Lips brushed hers. "Accept me."

How could she live with herself?

"I feel you getting wet, so stop shaking your head no. Talk to me and tell me."

So he could counter with endless arguments? So he could weasel his way deeper into her guts?

"Use your words, Eugenia."

"Please… I'm begging you not to come in me."

His answer was a roll of the hips, his cock dragging awfully until her fluid caught and female lubrication cut the burn. He thrust into her slowly, watching her face as she went through the kaleidoscope of madness that came with mental and physical brutality.

“You’re the most beautiful thing I’ve ever seen in my entire life. You feel so good, so right.”

But all she felt was grief.

And he knew it, answering her sucking breaths on each thrust with an adoring smile. “You’ll get used to it. You’ll adapt, you’ll learn. The perfect student.”

Slowly, like his cock sinking into her body, butting up against a fertile womb, it sank in. “I’m going to die on this boat.”

With that, he came, his mouth open, face twisted in ecstasy. Eyes holding hers through every kick and spurt as he filled her. And then his head fell to her shoulder, where he began kissing her, where he wrapped his arms around her body. Where he said, “Old and comfortable. Surrounded by our grandchildren.”

“Locked down on Level 9.” This was real. All of it was real.

Sleepy, he nestled. His too-big dick still buried. “I’ll make you happy. I swear it.”

# Chapter Thirteen

The ice pack wasn't optional.

Stunned from what Aaron had just done to her, in broad daylight, as it were. From all he'd just said, Eugenia lay there and couldn't grasp how it had gone so far. And like he always did, he took advantage. Tucking a pillow under her head. Taking inventory of all the battle scars he could find. Replacing Band-Aids, kissing booboos.

He even inspected between her legs where his seed leaked free. Seed he caught up with a finger and put back in with a smile.

Swollen, bruised, he'd told her. But no blood. That last virgin blood had been spilt the prior night, pink smears on the sheets.

The towel Joan had wrapped the ice pack in was soft, laid between the limp thighs of a defeated woman. Chill cut the throb. But the broken heart under her ribs?

There wasn't going to be an easy fix for that aching organ.

"Do you want your textbooks? I know you like to sleep with them when you're upset."

Turning away from him, legs closing on the ice pack to keep it where it served a purpose, she tucked her face into the pillow. "Knowing you've been watching me sleep is really unsettling."

"You knew I was in the room."

Yes. She had known. And it was nice to have those long silences in the dark where she didn't have to be alone. Where he never made her talk. Where he rarely did more than sit on her mattress, elbows to his knees.

Where she'd known he'd left another woman sleeping on his couch or in his bed.

Covers were pulled over her aching body, and then her beloved books were set beside her hands.

"Sleep will do you good." A gentle hand landed on her curls, stroking mussed hair from her face. A gentle voice, southern to the core, petitioned,

"I'm asking you not to do anything that might harm yourself or anyone else on board while I'm gone. No fires, Eugenia. Arrangements need to be made, work done, but I'll be back by dark. If you get hungry, Joan left food in the bags. If you get thirsty, there's water. All your things are here if you want to unpack. And I prepared a present. Several new textbooks—my personal favorites back from my teaching days—but most are medical in nature. You'll find them in the cabinet under the bar."

She ignored him.

Buttoning up his jeans, he said, "We can go for a walk on the deck when I get home."

Like a dog being let out so it wouldn't shit on the carpet.

"Change is never easy, Eugenia, but it's going to be okay. I promise." A kiss landed on her forehead.

And then he was gone, unlocking and then locking the door.

Dreamless sleep stole in—the kind that keeps the desperate and the broken alive. Sucking fragmented fools so deep they fought waking.

But a hand jerked her shoulder. “Young lady, that’s enough of that.”

Groggy, burrowing under the covers to escape the utter annoyance, Eugenia growled, “Go away, Mom. I’m tired.”

“And you’ve slept enough. Sleep all day and you’ll never sleep at night. So get up.” Off went the covers, the air-conditioned breeze drawing Eugenia into a hissing, sore ball. “You’re going to take a shower while I change these sheets.”

Brushing matted curls from her face, Eugenia found her wits. “For Christ’s sake, Joan, what the fuck are you doing?”

Already pulling at the bottom sheet, glaring, Joan said, “*You* a world of good.”

That bitch had done enough *good* already. “I’m tired. Go away.”

"You're depressed and moping. And you stink. Go take a shower and cook up one of your creative comebacks. When you're done, put on the dress hanging on the door and join me for a bowl of strawberries and a shot of vodka. Lord knows I need it after last night." The woman kept on tugging dirty fabric, as if she'd unmade and remade this bed a dozen times, muttering under her breath, "The pair of you kids both need a hard knock upside the head."

It was either get off the bed or be rolled off, so she moved. But she did it with several curses. All the while, watching the muttering woman continue to castigate both the captain and Eugenia.

"He doesn't know you're in here, does he?"

"Of course not!" Bob swinging, Joan abandoned her work to glare at the naked woman. "Shower. Move it."

Bossy much? "I don't know what you think you're pulling—"

"No! I don't know what *you* think you're pulling, young lady." Circling the bed to chastise her properly, Joan snapped, "It's plain as day that you're as in love with him as he is with you. He might not have figured it out yet, but don't think you're fooling me."

"Excuse me?" Was this woman off her meds?

In a broad sweep, Joan pointed to the suite's bathroom. "Stop sputtering at me and go shower."

Fine. Shower, clean sheets, get the woman out of the room. FINE!

Walking with an embarrassing aching lady-parts gait, Eugenia abandoned the cleaning tornado to hose down.

Warm water eased hurts. Clean teeth livened the mind. Smelling like herself, and not like the aftermath of too much sex, did help.

But only so much.

When the faucet turned off and a towel hit sore skin…

Eugenia was stuck.

Stuck staring.

Apparently, stripper clothes they had by the hundreds, but regular dresses were hard to come by. Leaving her option the same blue dress from months back, bloodstain gone and buttons replaced.

There was no lacy underwear.

Which was just fine. Abused skin needed to breathe.

Red curls wet and drooping, left eye black and swollen, lip cut, bruises just about everywhere, Eugenia looked in the mirror and saw how much older she'd grown. No longer a fresh-eyed girl ready to take on the world.

Now all woman. One who'd learned that the world bit back.

Shivering in the air conditioning.

The door muffled Joan's holler. "Are you coming, or am I drinking this vodka by myself?"

Eugenia had barely been old enough to drink when the bombs fell. And now sperm might be meeting egg in her fallopian tube where an embryo would bounce around for days on its journey to the uterus… and a midwife was offering her hard liquor.

Hard liquor Eugenia was absolutely not going to turn down.

Bathroom abandoned, she found their positioning was all wrong. Joan had taken Eugenia's seat, leaving Eugenia to sit where the captain would sit. Not that she was going to say anything, but it felt backward.

Sitting in general felt uncomfortable.

"Drink up." They clicked tumblers, Joan adding, "I can get you more ice if you need it."

Swallowing the whole thing, blowing air from pursed lips, it took Eugenia a moment to ask what Joan's expression made it clear they both knew was coming. "Can you get me off the boat?"

Topping off Eugenia's glass with another splash of vodka, the older woman curled her lip. "Yes, but I won't. You do test my patience to no end, but that doesn't mean I want to see you dead. And that's all that's out there, young lady."

Glancing over her shoulder out the captain's floor-length windows to the rotting woods, Eugenia asked, "But there's gotta be somewhere good, right?"

"You remind me so much of my daughter. She had her head in the clouds too. Such a dreamer…" A sad smile, a wistful sigh. "Avery was in LA shooting a pilot—sure she'd be the next big thing. No one who knew her would have doubted it for a minute."

Vodka worked its magic. Or maybe it was that view, or the company, or the general fucked-upness her life had become. "I'm not sure what to say to that."

"It's a big ship, Eugenia."

"Someone else phrased it in exactly those same words."

"Tennis and basketball courts, multiple running tracks, playgrounds, three theaters, a massive promenade—every part repurposed to maintain and protect life. The conference center is now a classroom. There's a medical bay—"

Eugenia raised her hand. “I get where you’re going.”

“I don’t think you do.”

“He forces women to have babies whether they want to or not.”

“He does.” Joan sipped her vodka.

“And you help him.”

Without a blink, she said, “I do.”

“And those little girls on board, the ones in the school or playing games with the little boys at recess, how are you going to explain it to them when they grow up and get dragged to the nightmare on Level 15? How are the boys going to feel to trade tickets to fuck their childhood sweetheart?”

“Have you ever noticed that nature tends to correct itself. Most of the babies born since the fall are female. There is almost an even spread between genders.”

That was mildly fascinating. “Those same little girls will one day grow up and be forced to carry babies they might not want. What if they’re gay?”

“Insemination? There are options we can discuss—”

“Please.” A tipsy eye roll matched Eugenia’s disgust. “Oh, and how about who gets matched with whom. What about love?”

“You found it, and you’re already spoiling the gift, so maybe try another topic.”

Eugenia was about to chuck that lead crystal tumbler right in Joan’s face. It sure would fuck up the woman’s well-done facelift. “I don’t know where you think you get off!”

“You’re even lying to yourself, Eugenia.” Joan sipped from her glass. “I’ve seen the way you look at him.”

“Yeah. Like I’m planning his murder.”

“I’ve seen you two sneak off together.”

“To argue.”

Mirroring the sass, the obstinance, and the tone, Joan laid it all out. "Fine. You're not in love. Tell yourself that if it gets you through the day. But you are good for morale. You cannot imagine the burden that man carries. The responsibility and tough decisions."

"He's a sociopath."

"The pure fact that he loves you and announced it to the entire deck last night contradicts that statement. Sociopaths don't feel emotion."

"Okay, then he's just evil."

Joan didn't even try to argue that one. "Only because he has to be."

"Ha. Gotcha. You agree he's evil." Grinning, Eugenia sipped her liquor, feeling cocky, feeling warm. "I win." And then it sank in. "Wait, did you just say he announced that he loved me to the deck? Has he lost his mind? The women will rebel. Scarlet has it bad for the prick. So does Faith."

An overgrown eyebrow that would have been perfectly waxed into an arch when salons were on every corner, lifted. "Why do you think I'm drinking today?"

"Should I anticipate more glass in my food?"

"You're not going to be allowed back to the party. No need to flaunt what the others can't have." After an extended sigh, Joan added, "And to be frank, I'm not sure he'd ever let you near the men again."

"So it's to be chains and some breeding post on Level 9 after all."

"There's an issue with that as well."

That deserved a snort. "Only one?"

Settling back, legs crossed at the ankle, Joan sighed. "I'm fresh out of chains. Any suggestions on alternatives? Twisty ties?"

It had to have been the vodka; there could not possibly be another reason for the pair of them to burst out laughing as if they were friends.

Toasting, Eugenia raised her glass. "Joan, you're creepy and dark and… a little bit funny."

"If you gave him reason to trust you, I bet he'd let you come and go as you please." An amendment was added, after Joan smacked her lips, "So long as you avoid the men's decks, for obvious reasons. Reasons we both know I don't need to spell out."

"Tempting fate isn't so wise these days, is it?" Fully aware of what reason might make him trust her, Eugenia tried not to think of the potential sperm-meets-egg moment that may or may not have been taking place inside her. "Not that he'd take a chance on me getting off the boat. We both know I'm not going to be strolling the decks anytime soon, at least without a leash and a muzzle. Did he mention to you that my reward for not burning the boat down after he left was my very own walkies?"

Joan winked. "Woof."

"Ha-ha, old lady." Only it wasn't funny anymore.

"I'm sure he'll give you the nicest room, a pretty view. I'm also positive you won't be given a balcony."

Grin mean, Eugenia gestured to the grandeur of the captain's suite. "You mean I can't stay in here? But of course that's what you mean. That's why you're really here, winning me over with alcohol and fresh fruit." Taking a bite of a juicy strawberry, mouth full, Eugenia was frank about the rest. "He's not going to like your aspirations one bit."

Setting down her glass to get down to business, Joan met her eyes. "Will you help me convince him?"

"To keep to the schedule of fucking the Level 15 ladies?" Wow. He would hate having to continue to do his duty to them just as much as they hated, in many cases, doing their duty for the crew. "You have a mean streak, Joan."

"Baby steps. Change of this sort can't happen overnight just because the captain wants it to. The girls all want the same thing now. To have one man.

The men will want the same. If the crew sees that he's not faithful, the hurt will be less. Chance of another major incident will decrease."

"What was the incident?"

"Faith tried to hang herself."

"That's… I'm sorry."

"You won't have to see it, or talk about it, or know about anything that might happen in this room. And I think we both know he'll wash up and come right down to you." Joan's eyes pointed at a flat belly covered in blue cotton. "To both of you."

Scratching her cheek as she thought through potential scenarios, Eugenia scowled. "Assuming you abscond me to Level 9, I wouldn't even know what he did or with whom up here. Why even ask me? He could be fucking someone right now, and I'd never know."

"Because you have to be the one to make him do it. The captain wants to keep you in this room, and that… is a dangerous idea."

Objectively, the concept was fascinating—torturing him by making him fuck the others. But subjectively… "If I really loved him, my answer would be no."

Joan smiled. "I had expected your first objection would be germs."

"Then you should have considered that it would be easier for me to escape from an area of the ship I know than the heavily guarded *family quarters*. I don't give a shit if he fucks every last hole on this ship. I just want off the boat."

The question hung between them, Joan all-business. "And what if I offered you that?"

"I thought you said I'd die out there."

"You will. And that will be on you. A whole lot more people will die if there is unrest. So, even though I like you, I'll help you commit suicide."

Joan was a coward who hid on a whore ship and assisted in unspeakable acts against women's personal freedoms. What the fuck did she know about survival? Vodka and goddamn strawberries….

Eugenia would seek out her future just fine. “Swear it to me. You swear to me that if I play your game—”

“I’ll get you off the boat.”

Progress was made, the knots in Eugenia’s belly loosening. “If I find out you lied, I’ll kill you. We both know I will.”

Smiling, Joan held out her hand. “It’s a deal.”

The shake was firm; it was promising. “Pleasure doing business with you, Joan.”

# Chapter Fourteen

"You know this is a completely ludicrous idea!" Joan was right—the captain really was out of his gourd. Eugenia gawking at the single table set on a private deck, with candlelight and dinner waiting. "If anyone saw—"

"Who's going to tell them?" As if courting danger was nothing but a taste of fun, the captain pulled out her chair. "Sit. It gets a shade cooler on this side of the ship with no rock face to warm it."

All this said as he wrapped her in a blanket. Because, yes, it was cold.

And the candles were flickering, and the food… it smelled a whole lot better than the slop she ate day in and day out. Usually, Eugenia only got to watch other people eat like this, unless she conned one of the crew into giving her a bite for free.

After taking the chair across from her, he nodded at the food. "Go ahead and eat."

But it felt… completely against the rules she'd adjusted to. Rules that had grown comforting in their familiarity. "I'm not sure I'm hungry."

"Indulge me." His grin grew, roguish and self-possessed. "Or are you going to keep shaking in your boots?"

Brow cocked, she gave him a glare and picked up the fork. *And knife*.

The man was pretty damn sure of himself to give her a knife. And she couldn't help but laugh, looking down at the serrated edge and the polished glean of stainless steel. Using it to cut flaking fish that had no need for a knife… felt foreign. But she did, preparing a forkful covered in some kind of herb sauce.

And took a bite.

Understanding what he was saying loud and clear.

He wasn't afraid of her temper. Or that she'd tried to kill a man the day before. Or that even in that moment she watched candlelight play off the blade and considered if she could stab him before he might stop her.

Distracted by such thoughts, Eugenia muttered, “Who’s going to shoot you in the back of the head, I wonder?”

“Thinking of Neil?” Such manners, such suave smiles. Where was the lazy cowboy, and who was this stranger?

“He got what he wanted. You said you’d never seen him happier. And then that was the end of him.” This person was a stranger. One she looked dead in the eyes. “No one gets to be happy in this world, on this ship… not even you, I think.”

Daring to lean closer, to put his fingers on hers, the captain said, “I’m happy right now.”

“And I have a knife in my hand.” And his wrist was right there. She was looking right at it.

“One I hope you’ll use before your dinner gets cold.”

How he could pour it on thick, knowing just how low to drop that southern drawl to make her shiver. Shaking off his touch, needing both hands, another bite of fish went to her lips.

Yet, once her hand went down, his touch came back. "I've been thinking of ways to make you happy too."

"Oh, this should be good. Let's hear them, cowboy." She shook off his fingers again. "Considering the stellar job you've done over the last six months, I anticipate excellent dinner entertainment."

Playfully wounded, his eyes glittered in the dark. "We've had some fun here and there."

"True. I really enjoyed breaking your fancy dinner plates."

"I think that's when I first knew I loved you." He took a sip of water, wine conspicuously not on the table that evening. "Don't get me wrong. There was something the moment when you stared up at me on the dock. I wanted you then like I've never wanted anyone. But when you had your hair tied up, humming as you scrubbed. The way your cheeks got pink to be caught. Even that cute scream. I loved you that moment to the point there was no undoing it."

"Men don't talk like this." How she wished her words would have come out less breathless.

"I do. To you."

Whatever this was, she was going to put an end to it. After all, he'd given her a knife. "Aaron, you can cut the seduction routine. You already fucked me."

His correction was paired with a sinister smirk. "Made love."

"I wouldn't know the difference. It sure felt like I was being fucked." As in fucked over. Which brought out that very color to her cheek he commented on.

That made him laugh.

Shoving the rest of the fish in her mouth to make a point that she'd had enough of whatever *this* was, Eugenia said, "Well, this was exceedingly domestic, but I'm done. Let's get the fucking over with so I can ice my swollen crotch and go back to sleep."

"No sex tonight." He took a bite of fish, chewing slow.

"How are you going to get me pregnant if you don't—"

"Fuck you?" Another slow bite of fish, the captain taking his sweet time after interrupting to answer. "There's no rush. There's also no doubt that I'll get to watch your belly swell with my baby. Boy or girl, our kid will be perfect, and you will be beautiful."

Too much by far, she crossed her arms over her chest and got out of his reaching range. "Planning for me to whelp the next governor of Mississippi?"

That set him laughing. "Maybe a doctor."

Low blow. Faking an obnoxious yawn, Eugenia said, "My vagina hurts and I hate you, so let's wrap this up. You got duties, and I'm tired."

Up went that dark brow. "Duties?"

"Pretty sure it's your night with Faith. Don't keep her waiting on boring doggy style or an animated blowjob while she fingers herself to the taste of your cock. Since you can't look her in the eye, maybe show her that tongue thing."

The playfulness, the smoldering looks, all of it evaporated until the man she knew returned. "Who were you talking to?"

"I've been talking to you, and eating fish—which was good, by the way. Since my mother raised a lady, I will even say thank you."

"Don't play word games with me, Eugenia."

Grinning, she enjoyed the hell out of his burgeoning annoyance. "But it's fun… and you did say you'd been thinking of ways to make me happy. Seeing that look on your face is making me pretty darn happy."

Dangerous anger, that was the look. The temper he tried so hard to hide behind lazy smirks and stolen touches. "The only woman who will ride this cock is you."

She wasn't lying when she said she was having fun. The only fun around the ship was at his expense. "I'm flattered. I'm also not interested."

So he doubled down. "I said I wouldn't fuck you tonight. But that doesn't mean that now I don't plan to tie you down and do the tongue thing until you apologize."

Lady parts clenching at the thought, Eugena's smile fell. There was no way she'd be able to stand it. "Try to tie me up and I'll kick you right in the face."

The slow stand from his chair, how he leaned over their intimate table and grinned... it was demonic. "I'll risk it."

The man must have been some kind of rodeo champion in his past life. Throwing her over his shoulder, he hauled her to his room. Her back hit the mattress, each limb secured while she spat curses and shrieked.

One kick landed, square on his chest. One kick that left him laughing when he caught her flailing foot and secured it so she was spread. Spitting mad, she fought, unable to even reach the knots at her wrist—annoyed that she recognized the brand of tie and knew they must have been his.

Accusing, and angry, and desperately irritated it took her so long to realize it, Eugenia condemned, "You were on this cruise when the bombs fell. That's why all this personal shit is here!"

Pleased as punch, he licked his lips. "Always so smart."

"And this was your room. You've never even been out there!"

Lifting up her skirt as if unwrapping a present, he looked down at her pussy and hummed. "Oh, I've been out there. Where do you think I found my crew?"

Before she might do more than snarl and squeal, he fell upon his dessert. The tongue thing focused on her clitoris, one exposed when he pulled back her hood and teased until she writhed. Abraded labia and aching vagina were left in peace… but her clit was tormented until she came, furious and winded.

Wrists on fire from fighting the bonds, emotions askew as she stared at the ceiling, Eugenia understood that he tied the other girls up in the same fashion. On this bed. In this room. That the man who claimed to love her had been serviced every night for God only knew how many years.

And that she should feel something about that.

Lips and chin shining with her fluids, he prowled over her. Grin in place, he urged, “Say you’re sorry or I’ll do it again.”

Looking at the knot binding her wrist, in no mood for fighting, she sighed. “I’m not sorry, and you won’t do it again, because I’m asking you not to.”

Taking her chin so she might be made to look, his wicked tongue traced his lips in a perfectly filthy way. “Is it a real ask or are you being coy?”

“It’s a real ask.” She could not take another orgasm like that.

“Can I come on your tits?”

Had he really just asked her that? After all he'd done? And was he already unbuttoning her dress? "Go come on Faith's tits."

"So that's a yes." Popping the top button of his jeans, he shucked them off while somehow still managing to find his balance atop her. Then reached right on in and scooped out her breasts, Sandwiching his ridiculous cock between pale mounds.

Leaving Eugenia with a view of tan erection poking from squished boobs. His glans exposed as the foreskin caught with each thrust. As he fucked her breasts, unabashed, nothing but a beast.

Muscles rippling, he let go. He enjoyed. Watching her, clenching his ass to move his monster through a fleshy grip, base to tip… so near her mouth she could almost taste him.

In no way in a rush, he *enjoyed* her.

"Open."

Why on earth she did, she couldn't say, jaw wide as he splashed the first spurt of his spend on her waiting tongue.

The rest was smeared between her tits, slicking his way as his eyes rolled back and his back arched.

It was the sexiest thing she'd ever seen in her life.

His total loss of control.

On the last pulse, the one that came after all his seed twitched between her mashed cleavage, he looked down and said it again. "I love you."

And it was too much. Tasting come for the first time in six years, remembering how much she loved it. The intimacy of accepting something *a little dirty* on her lips.

"Hey." Stroking her cheek, the captain murmured, "It's going to be okay."

Terrified, because it never would be, she said, "I don't think it is."

"You'll see." After a sexy smile, he reached over, untying one sailor's knot and then the next. Rubbing her wrists where they were red. Kissing her fingertips. “I’m going to do the tongue thing again, nice and slow.”

Which seemed a particular mercy, her clit throbbing to be touched after that show. The traitor.

Her ankles still bound, her thighs forced open, he ate her pussy for ages. *Nice and slow*, her fingers in his hair, his grip cradling her hips. Riding his mouth, she took as he had taken.

The second climax washed over her—difficult, beautiful, dangerous—undulating from core to toes. The hardest she’d ever come.

Legs set free, he scooped her into his arms, rubbing her back and hushing her when the occasional sob escaped. The harder she fought to hold in the sound, the more often breath stuttered and her tears leaked free.

He told her to just let go, promised her that he’d help her through it.

She didn’t let go. No, she fought all she felt. So it burst out on its own until she was completely wracked by sobs.

While he whispered secrets to her in the dark—secrets about life, about the nature of humankind, about how he'd never, ever let her go—she fell asleep.

Utterly spent, hollow, and overfull.

# Chapter Fifteen

"Those things I mentioned. The things to make you happy…" Kissing behind her ear, urging Eugenia to wake with the heat of his body and the attention of his mouth, the captain said, "Today, I'll introduce you to the children."

Like a bucket of cold water to the face, Eugenia's heart picked up, her body tensed, and any hint of lazy drowsiness evaporated. "You're going to take me down to Level 9 and lock me in."

He didn't deny it. "I should…"

Considering Eugenia's standing agreement with Joan, her sharp, twisting fear should not have been allowed to leave her shivering. But if Joan was lying, and Eugenia was conveniently stashed away, it would only be a matter of time before the captain fished another *pretty girl of a certain age* out of the water. And where would that leave her?

It would leave her locked in a glorified breeding pen.

Candlelight dinners and orgasms—pockets of solace—didn't last. Nothing that had passed between Aaron and herself could be real. She knew that, yet when they were in bed, it was easy to forget. He was right. She was starving, and between the enlivening arguments, there had been something almost peaceful.

"I thought you'd at least wait until I was pregnant before you dumped me in your hellhole." Not that she intended to let that happen. Yet… she'd been unable to stop him from ejaculating inside her. She even enthusiastically participated in sex despite knowing what he'd do when his climax was reached.

Being alone with him was doing things to her mental state that were both dangerous and unsettling.

It was confusing her.

When he moved inside her, when he said sweet things, it was almost like she could forget the rest of it—exist only in the moment and pretend the other moments didn't matter.

But they did matter.

On Level 9, women were truly separated from any hope of freedom. Eugenia could see it in her mind's eye—the final door slowly closing before her. If she didn't run before he dragged her down there, she'd miss her chance to find the *good place* waiting out there.

And when she ran, she'd leave those women behind… knowing she'd abandoned them to save herself.

It wouldn't be the first time. After six years, the things she'd seen, each time adrenaline had pumped her legs to run faster, run farther, to not look back.

She felt it then, the skin-stinging anxiety that had become her new normal since the bombs. The shame.

As if he too felt the sting, the captain rolled away, leaving her body bereft of his heat and weight. Heading to the bathroom, he called over his shoulder. "No, you won't be permanently locked in. You'll learn the ropes of Level 9 in the day. Your nights will be spent in this room with me."

His nights were not available. Not when the captain's presence oversaw the raucous party where beer flowed and women relied on someone to maintain the rules. Not when his rotating schedule existed so he might fuck them all from behind and suffered for it, *as he should.*

And did he really think he could just throw her in the hole and pull her out at night when he wanted to play with her? Absolutely not! "Who's going to service Table #2?"

Chuckling from his bathroom, clearly urinating from the sound of it, he pitched his voice so she might hear from the distance. "New girl came yesterday. You've been officially replaced."

It shouldn't have hurt to hear. It shouldn't have hurt at all. But it did.

It hurt way down deep.

Cutting the anger and twisting it into sorrow, stealing her fuel for battle.

That was Eugenia's table, her chessboard, her ongoing fight against the machine. Would the new girl bend over and take it on her first night? Would there be anyone out there reminding the crew how fucked-up the whole show was.

Would the new girl cry when they dumped food on her head?

"How many tickets is she worth?" And how vile was it that she had to ask the man returning to bed that question?

Kissing the tip of her nose, the scowl between her brows, his voice was only consoling. "Not twenty-million."

There was a rattle behind Eugenia's heart, a strange fluttering both foreign and uncomfortable. A sensation that only grew worse when she looked him in the eye to suggest, "Give her some time before you put her on rotation for this room. I know you think I'm joking, but you're scarier than you'll admit. And don't jam your fingers in her on her first night."

Like steel shutters falling to hide what churned inside, the captain went back to the lazing, false cowboy. Utterly guarded, giving nothing away, he toyed with her hair. “Tell me what you’re thinking.”

“I just said what I was thinking.” No lie hid in those words. “And maybe… maybe don’t fuck them so hard. They don’t like it, Aaron. And I know you’re going to say you do that on purpose—”

“Just stop right there. I hear what you’re saying.” By the indifferent feel of him, it seemed he more than heard it.

Breathless in a way that ached, she shook her head. “I don’t think you do.”

“I do. I hear it.” Pulling the sheet over her breasts, he tucked her in. “You’re scared, and you don’t trust me.”

Who would? There wasn’t even a reason to shy from the subject. “I made a mistake trusting John. I won’t make it again.”

Lifting her hands, he kissed her finger. "You've been let down. You've been hurt."

So many times. "By you."

"From your perspective, I'm sure you've felt let down by me on more than one occasion," he conceded. "But I know, *I know*, Eugenia, it was all done in your best interest."

They'd always been honest with one another, but that didn't mean they had been honest with themselves. Eugenia needed him to recognize that. "No, Aaron. It was done in yours. Every favor you ever granted me has always come at a price. Every drop of blood I spilt on this boat was because of you."

Sprawling at her side, his weight on his elbow, he tripped his touch across her collarbones. "It's the eternal question of want versus need. I know what you want. My greater concern is with what you need. You often disagree, but here you are, healthy, safe. When the dogs howl, it no longer sends you crashing from your bed. You don't cry in your sleep anymore."

At no time was she going to discuss how often he came to sit in her room in the dead of night. Knowing he might have been there more often than she realized… made her uncomfortable. “You’re still the villain in the story. You’re not the hero because I got used to a mattress and shelter. I can decide for myself what I need.”

What she needed was to be away from tender touches and manipulative men with horse cocks and *the tongue thing*.

Spoken sweetly, as if he really cared for her, the captain said, “Then tell me what you think you need. I’ll listen, and we can discuss.”

Eugenia needed off the captain’s ship to run free without knowing she’d left women behind to suffer. “You should have never told me about Level 9. The reasons you did were revolting, Aaron. Don’t think that I don’t see the unwinnable crusade you’re trying to tempt me with. You want me to fight back so I’ll have a reason to stay. But I can’t save them from you. I’m not even going to try.”

Patient, he stroked her arm. “What else?”

The bait was right there, dangling. An offer to vent her complaints that would lead her nowhere, yet still, she spoke. “You came in me without permission. Held me down afterward so I couldn’t…”

“You knew by that point it was too late. Why should I let you run to the bathroom in a panic? Holding you still meant you had to consider. Which you did. And then I made love to you again, and held you down again. Like the wild dogs that used to send you running into walls in the dark, it’s a matter of adjustment and the slow realization that you are safe and everything is okay.”

There was too much to address in his statement with a single reply, so she changed tactics. “The first night we met, you struck me, put your hand around my throat, and tore my hymen with your fingers. It hurt.”

He took a moment, even looked away as if deep in thought before replying. “My reasons for doing it won’t be adequate, so I concede. I wanted to touch you first, since I knew I'd have to wait to have you brought to my rooms. My reasons were selfish, and I believed John's graphic details of your sexual history."

"And right there, you summed up everything that is wrong with the society that you built. *You believed John.*" Saying so was oddly freeing and equal parts excruciating. The women had no voice, though they were the prize men desperately sought to attain. They had nothing but what the men decided they should have. "Even after the world ended, men have learned nothing. And thanks to you, on this *save the human race ship*, you created a system that reduced us down to nothing but a commodity. You're breaking the very women you expect to raise your children."

"That would be a historically accurate thing to say about the male population in general. But we outnumber you, and I've done my best to keep the ladies onboard secure."

Secure? Is that what he called it? "You whore them out for tattered bits of old carnival tickets."

“They can say no. You did.”

Her lip shook, because it wasn’t that simple. “You force them to breed on Level 9.”

He didn’t deny it. “Yes. A diverse gene pool and population growth are necessary to keep everyone on the ship alive. Not only for this generation, but for our children’s generation. And so on. The amount of work it takes to keep the machinery operating, to provide food, to protect the borders cannot be managed by a few. If we don’t leave the children a legacy that’s safe and ordered, they will scatter, and the work done here will have been for nothing. If we don’t give them enough diversity in potential mates, it won’t take many generations before the population will become inbred. Not everything can be about you, or about me, or about the women who I have sacrificed for the greater good, or even about the men enslaved by a herd mentality system they cannot break free of.”

“You’re an evil man.” Yet saying so tore her apart. It dragged her shoulders down, stole her gaze from his. It left her sitting up in bed with her knees under her chin as she stared at a boring bit of cruise ship art on the far wall.

Dragging red curls behind her shoulders, he spoke gently. “Make me a better one.”

God, his moves on the game board were expert, Eugenia afraid he might actually win. “I can’t.”

“Then take me the way I am.” Fingertips tripping down her naked spine, he added, “Enjoy a life with me where you will be better kept than any woman living in these times. I will give you children. Many, I hope, because I love kids as much as you do. I always have. Of course, there will be arguments, disagreements, and disappointment before the inevitable acceptance of your new life.”

“No.”

His slow stroke reversed, until his fingers might delve into her hair. Until he might pull her back down into his arms by her roots and make her look him dead in the eye. “Hear me when I say this. I do love you. So much so that your fear is justified. But it is also misplaced. You lack facts and always assume the worst."

Tucked in his embrace, she arched a brow. "Can you blame me?"

"No." The captain's mask slipped, Eugenia viewing a man in torment. "But you can't imagine how much I wish you'd have come to me willingly."

She couldn't bear to hold his gaze when he tricked her into seeing *him* and not the captain. It produced the worst kind of ache behind her ribs. "You could have asked me—"

"Don't be coy, Eugenia." A man could not have looked more lovesick. "I've asked. I've even begged."

Why was this killing her? "You said it yourself. Everyone has to pay."

The verbal gauntlet was lifted, the captain brushing her lips with his fingertips. "And I'll gladly pay. I'll take liberties, because I can. I will force you to stay safe on this ship, Eugenia." Firm, softness turning to iron. Even the quality of his voice became sinister. "I'm not asking anymore. From this point forward, I take."

And he drove home his point with a fiery kiss.

One that hurt when her torn lip was mashed against her teeth. A searing kiss that set her body aching when his arms squeezed too hard.

And he knew it hurt her.

The captain's statement was loud and clear; he *would* hurt her if he had to.

He was the glass in her food she was expected to eat with gratitude. An internal injury that would grow more painful as time passed until the pain in her guts inevitably killed her.

Pulling away, he left her lying on his rumpled sheets, Eugenia a pile of bruising and aches. He pulled away and went to fetch her aspirin and a glass of water to wash the pills down.

Helped her sit up. Apologized when she touched her stinging lip.

When the glass was drained, she set it on the bedside table. Such a normal thing to do in the most abnormal of situations. “Do you ever miss the howl of wild dogs?”

“No.” He produced a wide-tooth comb and began working the snarls at the ends of her hair.

Testing the swelling around her eye with careful fingers, she let him groom her. “The cracking sound the wind made when it rushed through dead tree branches—I miss that too.”

The comb’s teeth catching on a snarl, he sighed. “There is nothing but death out there, Eugenia.”

That could not be true, not on an intellectual level. Somehow, he had created life here. Someone else out there must have done the same. “Where do you get the meat to feed three-hundred-plus people? The vegetables? Farmland? Pastures? Steak doesn’t magically show up on a boat in the middle of a lake that stinks in the summer and is cold as fuck in the winter.”

The relief in his smile, it made the skin crinkle beside his eyes. "Nets for fish upstream. We rotate crops; men work the fields where we cleared forest to till. The good cuts of meat are only served to the men who earn passage to Level 15. Offal for the women who work there."

"Because it's more nutrient dense…" Which explained the mush and the metallic flavor.

"Children and mothers are given a balanced diet. Families are supplied with the best meat and harvest. Not every year is this bountiful. Wild dogs get at our chickens. Levees break or irrigation fails."

"You have communities off ship?" He'd have to. Otherwise, all their supplies would come from City, and the slave ship wouldn't be a secret anymore.

Nodding, he explained, "The men leave on rotation. No women. It's not safe. Believe me when I tell you that. Men in mass, when they find a lady outside the rules and structure… it can get ugly. The woman seldom survives it. And then we have to put down the men involved. There has to be tickets to urge them toward a prize more fun than a few nights raping a stranger to death."

Ice trickled down her spine. "Oh my God."

Softly, he pulled at a springy curl, observing the light and the fire. "But you've seen that, haven't you?"

Over and over and over. Been caught a time or two, or three, or four. Whether in a cage or outside it, she'd seen the remains of women who hadn't been so lucky.

Taking her hair from his fingers, tucking it behind her ear, Eugenia made a mental note to avoid farms. Which put a bit of a damper on her original strategy. Farm labor seemed like decent work, and a time or two she had found families working the land on their own. Living on their term and not friendly with strangers.

Bereft of her hair, the captain swept up her fingers as a replacement, weaving them with his own. "Shall we get dressed?"

Her attention left their entwined grip, landing on hazel eyes in an unfairly handsome face. “I’m not going down to Level 9. Sure, you can drag me. But you’ll have to break at least one of my bones to get me there. You’re not locking me in whether it’s just for the day or for forever. You’re not breeding me for tickets. I *want* to hear the wild dogs, even if they send me running from a bed of sticks and mud. I *want* to watch the trees rot. I *will* find a good place.”

“I see.”

But she wasn’t done. “Give me back to Level 15. Put me on the rotating schedule. I give you my word I will do my best to satisfy—even face-to-face—the few times a year I’m called to service you. I’ll lie to the rest of the women and tell them...”

“What will you tell them?” Spoken with the cold death of emotion.

“I’ll tell them that you fucked me too hard from behind. That I slept on the couch. That I blew you and no matter how hard I tried, I couldn’t get you to look at me.”

“And just what are you going to do on Level 15?”

The words came fast, betraying her shaky foundation. “Earn tickets. I know what you’re going to say. Brooke… she ran into trouble. But I’m smarter than she is. I always get out.”

He didn’t flinch, once again a stone wall of a man as he rose from the bed. “Then let me get you your map.”

Going to his closet, retrieving a clean pair of jeans, he pulled them on, unsmiling, as he watched her sit up in a pool of white sheets.

On went a shirt, a nondescript button-down.

Walking with purpose, he opened his door and closed it in an unhurried manner. The lock set in place with a resounding click.

Ten minutes later, a stranger who bore a terrifying resemblance to Brooke was led through the door. Cowering into herself. Dressed in a hospital gown.

A terrified, clinging stranger.

Gathering back long hair, the captain exposed the familiar face the girl tried to hide.

A face that had been mutilated—cuts left to close without proper suturing. Angry, infected, ghastly patterns.

Brooke hardly blinked.

His voice soft, the captain said, "Here's your map, Eugenia. Your advice to travel south toward Fresh Water. *You* gave her directions straight into the worst hive of violence in five hundred miles. Fresh Water is gangland. You did this to her, and if you leave, this is what will happen to you."

The verbal knife slipped through her ribs, straight for the heart. In horror, Eugenia drank in a friend. A woman holding on to the captain as if he might keep her safe. As if this was the *good place*.

Eugenia had enough medical training to understand the damage on display was never going to heal properly without repeated reconstructive surgeries. And surgery was not an option. She'd never gone that far in her medical training. "You let me give her the map."

Nodding, he tore out her heart. "The savages mutilated her genitalia. Her clitoris and labia were removed—the wounds seared shut the same night they began to rape her for sport."

Very little was more hideous than the concept of female circumcision. It was a forever rape—the total loss of ability to enjoy sex without a great deal of effort and proper mental stimulation. "I didn't know."

"Yes, you did." Letting Brooke's beautiful hair fall back to cover her face, the captain added, "You knew, because you have been out there for six years. You've seen this before."

Her reply was small, her chin quivering. "Yes."

"And you told all the women on Level 15 that there was a world out there worth living in. Fed them your talk of freedom."

"There has to be." There just *had* to be! This couldn't be it. Locked away and used to make babies. What of her mind? What of her ambition? "Somewhere has to be the way it was!"

"The world is nothing but savagery and violence." He almost seemed to pity her. "There is no life for you off this ship, Eugenia."

That was the last straw. His ploy, *his manipulation of history,* laying all the blame at her feet was wrong. "You whored her for tickets and let her walk off this ship, knowing what was south!"

"*You* gave her the map. You filled her head with possibility." Blunt patience and pity became anger. "And don't think I didn't try to stop her. Brooke had been given the option to transition straight to Level 9. But she had your map, and your misguided bullshit to see her to *freedom*. And look at her now."

No, Eugenia couldn't bear to look anymore.

"LOOK AT HER, EUGENIA!"

Startled by the soft-spoken man's yell, Brooke began to pee in submission like a spooked dog. And it didn't stop—the damaged girl's urine kept hitting the carpet.

In horror, Eugenia found she lacked the bravery to move from the safety of the captain's bed to help her. "Brooke?"

"Can I go home now?" The whisper for the captain, not for her.

"Yes, lamb." Pressing a kiss to the top of Brooke's bent head, his whole demeanor shifted to gentle. "Of course you can go home. I'll take you right back."

Guiding the shuffling female from the room, the captain didn't so much as look over his shoulder at the stricken redhead sobbing into her hands.

# Chapter Sixteen

Tears running down her cheeks, Eugenia pulled on her only dress.

Using the fine towels from the captain's bathroom, she blotted up the mess of urine. Urine that smelled of an unwell person.

*Do no harm*. The first rule in medicine.

Yet she had harmed Brooke. The advice had been well-meant. Eugenia had only suggested the exact same course she intended to follow once she made an escape: follow the map to Fresh Water.

Where John would have sold her to a far more hideous fate than serving drunken, horny men.

Over the years, all the credit she'd given herself for being smarter than everyone else. All the abuses she'd eluded.

Sheer. Dumb. Luck.

Spirited, determined Brooke was broken… Eugenia would have been broken too.

Was breaking.

A fissure ran through her spirit; it had been eating at her for years. Growing wider with each encounter, deepening with each escape. An aching throb of emptiness and loneliness that was only held together by tattered bits of hope.

And lies.

All the lies she told to herself so she might stumble through another day.

There was no *good place*. There was only survival or death.

There were only men who pushed too hard and stole pieces off the gameboard. Who broke the rules and twisted the sport. Men who were willing to subject dead women in living bodies to the trauma of pregnancy and childbirth they didn't want.

As if humanity deserved a fresh start. As if the transgression would disappear with a smiling new generation raised by mothers locked on Level 9.

Children devoid of fathers like Neil who only wanted to hold their offspring.

Neil who Eugenia knew had fathered at least one of the babies on the ship. He wouldn't have grieved the loss of holding a baby so much if he hadn't.

She hadn't known him well, but he'd seemed like a good man. Yet outside the ship, good men changed. They mutilated the genitals of women for reasons Eugenia couldn't even begin to grasp.

Even the captain's leashed men slipped. He'd had to put them down, he'd said.

The lock clicked, the door opening… Eugenia still cleaning up pee, grieving a million different things at once.

Brooke's mutilated mouth, her glassy-eyed stare… the reason her friend walked with so pronounced a limp. The unbearable guilt for thinking she'd find salvation in *saving* Brooke.

For knowing that as much as she hated it here, it was better than anything she'd ever found out there.

"I'll never love you. If you got me pregnant, I'll find a way to not be anymore."

Eugenia was poison.

Living in such close quarters, she had gotten to know the women on Level 15—the ship the closest thing she had to family in six years. And she couldn't bear it. She could not bear knowing she'd fed into their desire for freedom they'd never have.

She knew the men. She'd laughed with them, mocked them, yelled at them, belittled them for her own amusement.

She'd grown dependent on Aaron for mental stimulation and a sense of normality. She'd had sex with him and given over to the act. Enjoyed it even after she grasped how he'd tricked her.

Aaron who had no pity left. "Fine. Take off your dress. Get up on the bed. All fours. Don't look at me."

His disappointments weighed down upon her back, as if he'd been saving it all up for that moment.

The pain of it felt… familiar, because this new world hurt.

Or maybe at heart she was a masochist. Either way, Eugenia deserved what was coming. Which was why she was already lifting the two-day-old blue dress over her head. Which was why she went to the bed as if stumbling through a dream and assumed the position every Level 15 girl knew by heart.

Already up behind her, voice devoid of feeling, the captain ordered, “Spit on your hand. Rub it between your legs.”

Shifting to balance her weight so she might look at her palm, so she might try to make her dry mouth produce saliva, she obeyed. She smeared her opening.

Not that it mattered.

He was in—a solid thrust that lurched her body forward and snapped her teeth together.

Tangling his fist in her hair as if she might disobey and turn her head, he fucked her. Too hard. Too fast.

And it was awful.

But she bore it: his size, his coldness, the sting on her scalp.

How there were no comforting caresses or any type of intimacy.

And on it went, rocking her breasts forward, leaving her wrists aching so she might hold position in the onslaught.

He didn't come.

Releasing her hair, he took her hips. Pounded faster.

And when she couldn't take another moment of the captain punishing himself for the sins they shared, she braved a glance over her shoulder.

And found a man in abject misery.

A man who loathed every moment of friction on his cock.

Who'd screwed his eyes shut and thrown back his head as if concentration might make it end sooner.

"Aaron, stop." Softly said, full of pain for the both of them.

The mechanical pistoning of his hips slowed, those hazel eyes opening to the world he'd created—eyes bloodshot and aged by the hollow, terrible fissure just like hers that ate him from the inside out.

"Didn't I tell you to keep your head forward?"

She said it again, barely a whisper. "Stop."

His dick was half hard when he pulled out, when he marched naked to where she'd left her dress on the floor next to a pile of towels covered in human piss.

Picking it up, he threw it at her. "Sleep on the couch."

There were so many things she could have said.

*I don't understand what's happening between us.*

A lie. She knew exactly what happened. He'd offered her the best world he might create, cobbling it together despite ugly circumstances and personal loss. And she'd rejected it.

*Where is the man who wooed me last night?*

Gone, literally, barely having pulled up his jeans before he slammed the door.

*Please don't make me sleep on the couch. I can't be like them.*

Who would stop her from sleeping on the bed? No one. Because she was alone in the nicest suite on the ship.

But she lay on the couch anyway, naked, her dirty dress her blanket.

And Aaron didn't come home.

She knew, because there was no sleep. There was only watching the dark turn to light. There was a morning with no breakfast. An afternoon with only water from the tap to fill her belly.

And then an intrusion.

Thrilled, Joan barged in. “I don’t know what you did, but it worked! He spent the night and all day in Jessica’s room. Everyone’s talking about it.”

Eugenia would not throw up. She would not. “Then I’ve fulfilled my side of the bargain.”

Scoffing, Joan waved a hand. “I mean, it was only one night…”

Parroting the posture, the gesture, and the tone, Eugenia found solace in hate. “And I mean, it’s only one artery I need to cut.”

“Young lady.” As if that phrase might work…

“Old hag.”

Plucking an innocuous plastic keycard from her pocket, Joan dropped it on the floor. “This will open any door on the ship.”

It looked so bland, so anticlimactic as freedom lay discarded at her feet. “I’ll need water. Supplies.”

“I never said I’d give you that. You’ll die out there either way. Die sooner and save yourself the trouble of suffering.”

God, the woman really had a mean streak. One Eugenia felt was both enviable and a lash she deserved. “Like Brooke?”

Waving off the sting, Joan said, “The new girl is named Chrissy. She has red hair too. He always was one for a redhead. I’ll change the schedule so she entertains him tonight. Go while he’s distracted.”

Blue dress held to her chest, Eugenia came forward to swipe the keycard off the floor. “Won’t he know you gave it to me?”

“The door wasn’t locked when I came in. Far as he knows, you snuck out during the night and threw yourself overboard.”

Fair enough. “Which way do I go to get off the boat?”

That, Joan did assist her with, the verbal map set to memory, Eugenia pulling on a dress badly in need of a wash and setting off—in the opposite direction.

Joan was a liar. If she lied to her beloved captain, she was lying to Eugenia too.

But the key card did work, and as the sun set, level by level, on a massive ship designed to hold thousands, only three hundred men roamed. Men who were easily avoided as she wandered through what might be the home of a new civilization.

Cruise ships were generally tacky, draped in color and experience. While wandering, she found a dark casino, banquet halls with crystal chandeliers, guest rooms yet to be pillaged for supplies. Whatever she might find was stuffed into a pillowcase: pre-bombs cola bottles. Crackers wrapped in plastic way past their expiration date. Bags of nutritious nuts.

A proper pack lacking the familiar weight of written knowledge.

*Nelson's Textbook of Pediatrics, Volumes I and II*… she'd forgotten them on Aaron's bedside table.

Let the ship keep valuable knowledge. Let the doctors here learn from it.

Maybe the kids would benefit.

For heaven knew, she didn't deserve them.

Brooke's face and genitals were a testimony to that. The captain's broken heart payment enough.

Long past dark, a crisp breeze cut through her dress. Level 4—economy class rooms that were full of dust and smelled in need of an airing and boasted balconies. Standing in the wind, she heard the distant sounds of the Level 15 festivities, imagined she might even hear a search party, and dropped the small cabin's in-room refrigerator into the water below. Once the surface tension had been upset and chance of a severe impact injury massively decreased, she threw herself over. Simple physics. Landing feet first with not a single broken bone.

Pack dragging her down, the room's sofa floatation cushions strapped to her body buoying her up, the current had its way with her.

And for once, she didn't fight back.

Winter? Or was it spring? It didn't matter. Either way, she floated for hours, lips blue before she felt sediment under foot.

It was then she realized she had no shoes.

Dogs howled.

# Chapter Seventeen

Dress flaking with dried mud, Eugenia walked through dead woods. Meandering in no particular direction.

When she'd been closer to the ship, pockets of hidden farmland could be seen from the tree line. Acreage she would have once ran toward as a haven was now avoided at all costs.

Roads were circumvented on her lackadaisical journey to nowhere, leaving no staged corpses for her to loot. Which meant Eugenia's drinks had been exhausted, her snacks had been snacked upon. Weaponless, shoeless, and wild, she'd beaten the duck she ate for dinner to death with a rock.

Pre-bombs, duck confit had been one of her favorite dishes. As had duck breast sliced thin and served deliciously raw. Which was how she ate it off the bone.

Fire was not an option.

It might be seen.

And though that time of year in the south was chilly, it was nothing like the snows in Boston. The very ones that had driven her south to begin with.

Not that she wasn't cold.

Uncured skins from freshly killed vermin kept some feeling in her fingers and toes. Poorly tied together with little strips she'd carved through with sharp rocks, they covered her well enough. And stank.

That first week, the howls didn't wake her up like they should. Eugenia was too busy dreaming of hazel eyes, flashes of anger, the feel of a man's hands on her body. How he tasted.

Every woman on Level 15 knew how he tasted. He knew how they tasted. And she could only guess how many of them he'd been with since she cut and ran.

That was the price of her freedom, after all. Not that she ever imagined she'd earn it so quickly, or so unintentionally.

It was surprising how boring the days were when all she did was hunt and walk. Too much time spent remembering and too little spent thinking.

It was like she carried an infection and something even worse—doubt.

The women always came back, he'd said. But she couldn't do that, even if she'd caught herself walking toward the boat more than once. Seeing him with the others, the very women she'd driven him to time and time again, would kill her. It would kill her more quickly than Level 9 ever might.

Joan had been right. Eugenia was in love—unsure who she hated more for it, Aaron or herself.

Had Joan not come to her first, after that long, sleepless night on the couch, Eugenia would have fallen at his feet and begged just like he had begged her in dark corners for months. *Keep me. Accept me as fucked-up as I am. Love me back, even when I hate you.*

He'd outplayed her every move, crumbled her flagging resistance to powder. All the while, she'd tormented him in every way she could imagine. Took from his physical release despite his tricks. Participated when he'd moved inside her. Enthusiastically accepted his caress after a taste of pleasure, knowing after the first time that it would end with him spilling where he should not.

He'd take care of Brooke as long as Brooke might live. He'd take care of all of them. That had to be enough.

He'd also still force women who didn't want to have babies to reproduce for his vision of humanity's second chance.

Her best friend. Her arch nemesis.

Maybe she'd really left her beloved textbooks for him, so he wouldn't forget her. Because seeing them would kill him little by little. He'd hold them; he'd smell her on them. He'd still fuck the other women too hard from behind, and he'd still not be able to look them in the eye as they serviced their captain.

Brooke bore horrific scars, ugly ones everyone could see. Aaron bore the same, with only Eugenia knowing they sat right under his skin.

Just as he knew all about her secret wounds, having inflicted many of them himself.

Yet with each deep cut, she'd had someone to stitch the wound closed. The scar was still there, but tended, softened, even accepted. They only pulled a little when she breathed, could almost be ignored.

Eugenia would survive them. Aaron would survive his.

Neither of them would ever truly live.

It wasn't the cold or the hunger that birthed her misery in freedom. They wouldn't kill her, just as her growing fever wouldn't kill her. It was the loss.

Rain had blessed her passage from the ship with drinkable water. More had been collected in her empty cola bottles. She could pass from the rotting woods into the next nightmare far differently than she'd come to this land.

But the dead wood felt like home. So she built her own hovel out of mud and sticks like all other vagrants breathing air, eating bugs, and surviving on fumes she'd come across over the years. Eugenia's own cove near the water, far from the ship. Far from the captain's farmlands.

So she might work through a backlog of buried thought and feeling, yet occasionally wander far enough north in the night to see the ship's lights at a distance.

She wasn't alone.

Her beautiful Li Wei, his memory was with her, toasting marshmallows over a campfire she didn't have. Like he sat at her side on the muddy banks of the massive river that fed a lake that housed a cruise ship that should have never made it so far inland.

The Mississippi wasn't pretty.

Its inlets stank.

But so did she… in that stupid blue dress.

A dress she was going to keep until the day she died. Because she missed another man more than the ghost at her side. She missed all the ugly moments they shared punctuated by blue cotton.

Because she was sick.

Because she was broken.

Because all the women went back and she never would.

When the dogs finally ate her, she'd be wearing that dress.

Because the fact that Aaron might have been right about *everything* was too terrible to swallow down.

This, she told Li Wei; she told him everything. Sometimes crying, sometimes laughing, always horrendously honest. How much she missed him and the life they should have had. How angry she was that he left her as if he stood a chance at finding his parents. How much she envied him for loving so hard that he knew she would live without his help, but his Māmā and Bàba would not.

Sometimes, she railed as if the imagined phantom might reply, screaming out hateful things. How could he have left her? Didn't he love her enough to stay?

Of course he had. He loved her as much as any man had ever loved.

Even as much as Aaron loved her.

And Li Wei would have married her, and they would have been happy. But…

The world died, and men like Aaron lived.

Li Wei was too good; he would have been slaughtered protecting his wife. Aaron would have killed anything and everything that might even approach her.

Like Neil.

"I miss you." There had been a great deal of honesty in solitude, but that she had never dared mutter aloud.

Her new phantom answered back, "I shouldn't have done it."

Fever had grown worse by the day. A diet of bugs and weeds, of raw vermin and the occasional slow bird tended to do that.

Fallen log supporting her weight, Eugenia plopped down and stared as the world's ugliest river flowed past. "The bigger question is which *it* you mean. The slavery? The manipulations? Level 9? Fucking Jessica?"

"Jessica."

What was there to do but shrug then frown. "She's popular for a reason."

"I went to her room, traded her one-hundred thousand tickets."

Impressive when Eugenia thought about it—it even deserved a low whistle. "Wow, that's a lot more than I was ever offered…"

"I paid her to tell everyone I fucked her all night." The man took a deep breath, one so unlike the composed captain. "Instead, I got drunk on her balcony and passed out on her floor."

Standing on shaky legs, Eugenia approached the water's edge to pick up a flat rock and skip it over the tide. Eight skips before it sank.

"Eugenia. Did you hear what I said?"

How much she'd missed hearing the way Aaron said her name. As if there was no one else in the world but them. As if he really knew her… which he did. "I feel sorry for Jessica. She's been in love with Maxwell for years. He's been in love with her. But to hide it from you, they are always with other people."

"I know."

A sorry snort, and she started looking for a new rock to skip. "If you knew, both of them would be dead."

The specter's voice came nearer. "I know all of it, Eugenia. And I turn a blind eye when I can."

"That's… almost sweet." The real Aaron wasn't sweet. He was aggressive, relentless, unscrupulous, generous, beautiful, loving, and twisted.

"Going to Jessica was the cheap trick of a desperate man. One who knew you'd get off the boat one way or another. A man who'd tried everything he could think of to manipulate you into surrender. I left the room that night, because I needed you to be jealous, to be *anything* if you couldn't love me. Because *I was jealous* of everything you fought for. I'm jealous of the fucking ground you walk on."

This just might have been the most fulfilling fever dream she'd had yet.

Sane enough to remember that auditory hallucinations were a terrible sign, Eugenia looked down at the mud-stained, ugly blue cotton under her crusty furs. She'd lost weight. "I thought I'd die in a nicer dress, wearing the pearls my daddy gave me. I had never taken them off until the day I traded them for scraps, because it was that or pussy. God only knows where they are now."

"Honey, please look at me…"

Another perfectly shaped rock skipped over chilly waters, Eugenia smiling to beat her record.

"Shouldn't it be lamb? Lamb to the slaughter? Lamb on a spit? You called Brooke lamb."

Pain, there was so much pain from her ghost's confession. "I could have told her about Fresh Water, and I didn't. I needed a living example to open your eyes."

The tear that fell was warm on her cheek. "I know… but it wouldn't have mattered which way she went. There is no happy ending anywhere."

"Eugenia… please."

Closing her eyes to the sound of a stalwart man begging, she sighed.

But the phantom was relentless. "I would be happy to just be able to see you"—and the voice came closer—"even if you never let me touch you again."

"If we'd met in some bar before the bombs, if you'd approached with your swagger, your good looks, and your unbearable pretentiousness... I would have thrown my drink in your face."

There was amusement in the specter's reply. "I just bet you would have."

“Do you? Because I’ve thought about it to an unhealthy degree, and I’m not sure why.”

The amused lilt, she’d missed the sound of it. “Because I scare you. Because I’m brazen. Because I’m all the things you want but would never admit.”

“Those things are true, but I think it’s because with just one look, I would have seen exactly what you were capable of. Men like you ended the world.” A deep breath, the hard work of peeling her eyelids open accomplished, she prepared to turn and found nothing there. Cutting a glance to the side, she found his boots… badly in need of a polish. Running her eyes over dirty jeans, a flannel, a man in a coat, until she found the new beard growth on his face. “I know who you are, Kingston.”

Was that relief in his eye? “I know you do.”

“But we’ve never talked about it, not really.” God, she was a mess, covered in dirt, hair all snarls. Running a hand down her tangled mane as if she might knock the dust out, she said, “It’s the eyes, the cheekbones. You've got Joan's good looks, but deep down, you're all Daddy."

"Joan would be proud to hear that; it was her one job. Be pretty and raise an heir." Settling into his stance like a trained politician, the captain added, "Did she ever tell you she was runner-up to Miss America? Born and raised to be a politician's wife."

"And though Granddaddy might have been Governor, your father—"

"Was a senator." And the phantom didn't even have the nerve to look embarrassed.

"Not just any senator. An avid supporter of the crispy, dead president's untrained private police. The army he marched into cities to murder, arrest, and terrify the people rising up against his regime. A supporter of the war America started. Evil like you."

"I'm not my father…"

"Keep telling yourself that."

There was the familiar, irritated squint. "I'm not my father, because I would never settle for the senate when I could have had the oval office."

Which deserved mockery, considering. “What shape is your office on the ship?”

“Rectangular.”

“Hmm.” That was a little funny. “Your mom is afraid for you. What does it feel like to have a mom who is still alive and able to be afraid for their child? I miss mine. I miss her in a way I don’t know how to describe. Not just because she was hard on me, but because she was great.”

And Eugenia had meant *great* in the way that artists were great. The way countries were great. Her mom had been a juggernaut that had changed the world for the better. All that surgical knowledge gone forever, thanks to Aaron’s father.

The phantom took a cautious step closer. “Eugenia, what did Joan say to you?”

“She only told me the truth. You can’t have me and keep peace on the ship. And you know it too.” Since this was final confessions and all, she tacked on, “And though I do hate you, I couldn’t see your work fail just because the pair of us were…”

"In love?"

"Call it whatever you want. It doesn't matter."

Breathless, he looked torn apart. "It matters to me."

How many times did she have to tell him? "You don't get to be happy!"

"Why?"

A sob caught in her throat. "Because I am afraid of Level 9. What it means for the world. What it would do to me to allow it."

"I know," he said with such feeling, with so much love in those hazel eyes. "Which is why I am removing your ability to choose. There won't be guilt because I'm stealing you from the world. Because from this moment forward, I own you. And I'll remind you of it every day."

Was he crying? Phantoms didn't cry. This… this couldn't be real. "Aaron?"

Gesturing to the dead wood at his back, he waved forward. "Boys, tie her up."

# Chapter Eighteen

How different it was from the first time she'd seen those welcoming lights, their enticing sparkle suckering in wayward strangers. With her head cradled on Aaron's lap, the vantage was not a tempting glint of civilization from a crumbling stone bridge. She didn't need to squint to see what was hidden behind the trees.

Eugenia saw the ship clear as day, growing larger as the dinghy that carried her home was oared by strong men.

There was no John running to the shore, abandoning his pack and diving into murky waters.

There was only Aaron, stroking her hair all the hours it took the men to row upstream. There was only fever and raw wrists from fighting rope that bound her weak limbs.

But the ship looked the way she remembered from that first awful encounter.

Pretty, jovial, a beckoning finger in a world of rotting corpses.

*A bad place.*

Or was it a good place where bad things happened?

It was more than the men on the gangplank. The decks were full. Cheering abounded.

She heard her name shouted in homecoming. As if she belonged. As if she'd been missed.

"Hush now." Taking her chin, the captain turned her head so she might meet his eyes. So she would see his intention, his smirk… his victory. "You don't have a choice, remember?"

She didn't have a choice... so it was okay if she allowed a tiny pang of relief to bang against her heart.

That so long as she fought the ropes binding her wrists and ankles—so long as Aaron carried her over the threshold—boarding the ship might be okay.

Met with cheers, with triumphant waves, one would think the captain was bringing home his bride. Not some vagrant in a crusty dress that reeked of body odor and sickness. Cradled to his chest, marching them straight up that red carpet as if returning victorious from war, he brought home a woman they all knew.

One he wasn't going to share. To a crew and the Level 15 ladies that cheered anyway.

Dictators didn't ask if they could have what they wanted; they took it. And the regime didn't question.

Not when they were fed. Not when they had tickets to earn and ladies to entertain them.

Not when they could buy a cycle and potentially father a child.

Was it really so different than how it had been before society fell apart?

Powerful men's wives had been chosen from a myriad of pretty contestants backstage at the Miss America pageant. Now they were plucked from rancid lakes, trotted about in naughty catholic schoolgirl outfits, and made to stand still as men dumped their uneaten food on their heads. So really, pretty much the exact same thing.

The captain had put a ring on her finger once his men had tied her up, slipping it on after she'd quickly grown tired from struggling and ultimately lost.

And as her hands were bound before her, she could see the setting sun glinting off the gold.

It couldn't have been Joan's; it was too plain. Joan would have owned a monstrous diamond.

Plain suited Eugenia; the fucking band even fit, mashed between her fluttering fingers. As if he'd planned it all, the more she struggled, the more she felt it.

Aaron had called her his wife.

Solid muscle, holding her close, he whispered his vows on the muddy banks of the Mississippi. Gagged, she could do nothing but glare as he promised to keep her forever.

To chase her down if she ever got it in her head again that she belonged anywhere other than at his side.

To love her.

To see her fed and their children cared for.

Eugenia gave no promises in return. That wasn't how his world worked.

She could have promised to cut his heart out, and he would have still smiled, still kissed her forehead, still planted her on the waiting dinghy.

Because she didn't have a choice.

She didn't have a choice in the following examination once she'd been returned to the ship. She didn't have a choice when he cut off her dress, when he scrubbed her in a bath of cool water, or the clean sheets he laid her upon when she was too tired to fight back.

A man Eugenia recognized as a frequent of Table #2—the one who traded three beers for a win at chess—poked and prodded while Aaron held her still.

He even introduced himself. Dr. Herbert, who had sat at her table every single time he made it upstairs.

Three days of fever, the captain manning the bucket while she purged whatever she'd poisoned herself with while scrounging through the wood. Holding back her hair, telling her over and over that she was beautiful and strong. That she would get better. That everything would be okay.

Bedrest was followed by careful walks around the deck. Constant attention. Private dinners with candlelight. Quiet moments for her to settle in.

An utter lack of arguments. There was very little talking at all.

Eugenia didn't know what to say. For once, the captain didn't push.

No sex took place on his massive bed, only soft caresses in the dark. Sleep-tangled bodies and lazy mornings.

Her period came, Eugenia ignoring the cramps to face her captor and announce, "I win!"

He didn't mind the mess, pulling her to his chest to stroke her hair. "You do, honey."

The blood was right there. Right there on the sheet. And then it hit her, and the words sounded sad. "There's no baby."

"We can try again." Arms tightened, a firm body holding her still. "Don't cry."

But she did. She fell to pieces, and she didn't know why.

***

*Nelson's Textbook of Pediatrics, Volume II* was in her hands. Aaron was rubbing her feet. A dark, lazy night on the couch, Eugenia reading by candlelight.

With a thumb digging into her arch, an automatic bow to her spine, she fought the temptation to close her eyes and give over.

"Eugenia..." Playful, swiping his tongue over the tips of her toes, he called to her.

A very clear call for *something more*.

Plucking the textbook from her fingers, he cocked his lips. Away went valuable knowledge and on came a hungry male, prowling. Slow, efficient, in his conquering of the damsel on the couch.

The first kiss wasn't inquisitive. It wasn't searching. It didn't ask.

Not that she let him get away with it. Hand to his chest as if she had a dream of shifting his weight, she bit. And he laughed, biting her back until she yelped.

Her snarl followed with the captain knocking her book to the floor, working his knees between her thighs, and leaving her gasping when he rocked against her.

"No more putting it off." All growls, all husky moans, he worked his clothed hips between her legs. "No more pretending not to look at me then blushing when you get caught. No more teasing. No more pining."

"Do I climb on all fours and promise to keep my head forward?" The spite, it came through, Eugenia unsure if it was intentional or not.

Aaron's pain followed, though it was buried deep in a searching hazel gaze. "I want to see your face. You know that." Running the length of his pants-clad erection over her panties, his demeanor hardened. "Not that I won't make love to you that way when the mood strikes."

He always called it *making love*. Whispered about the things he would do to her in her ear as she woke, detailed exactly which part of her body he couldn't wait to *lick, suck, tease* when they showered.

Two weeks of readjustment and an endless sensual assault.

Ending now.

Because she was wet—he had that power. More importantly, he had that skill.

But so did she. One lingering look before he *went to work* and she'd leave him adjusting himself and cursing. Licking her lips when they dined on fish, on berries from Joan, overtly sexual and entirely cruel, she made him a simmering monster of need.

Need she refused to fulfill yet egged on with mean giggles and evil lip-biting.

That was their game.

Chase and take.

"Aaron?"

Drawl liquid, he said, "Yes, honey?"

No way was she going to allow him to set the precedent. Kiss-flushed lips to his ear, she whispered, "I never did teach Chloe my deepthroat secrets."

"Jesus."

"But I won't swallow you down unless you look me in the eye the whole time. Unless you say my name. Unless you come where I can taste it."

Rearing back, he said, "You're an evil woman."

Which left her laughing. Laughing as she pushed him to sit. Laughing as he fought his belt and zipper. As he shimmed out of his jeans and that incredible cock sprang free. Smirk in full effect, she lowered between his thighs and met the hungriest, most vulnerable of male gazes with a wink.

And then she made him suffer.

It might have been six years, but committed penetration virgins knew tricks most men could not imagine.

Drawing out his agony, swallowing around his girth, fondling parts of him that would send most men screaming from the sensation, she brought him to a climax that had him doing far more than calling her name.

Through it all, he held her eyes—exposed, in love, manipulative, evil, good, lonely, unrelenting man that he was.

Eugenia drank him down like wine.

When air became a necessity, she pulled off his cock with a loud pop to her lips and smiled.

“That was mean.”

Wiping her mouth with the back of her hand, she asked, “Does Chloe do it better?”

Narrowed eyes and an agitated groan were his answer. “Every man you’ve done that too… they are very lucky they are not on my ship.”

Which set her back to laughing. “It’s funny when you get jealous.”

As the topic of jealousy seemed to be the thorn that always irked him, the captain frowned. “Tell me you love me.”

Arching a brow, she challenged, “Do the tongue thing.”

“No.” There was her playful lover. The one who needed so much she might never fill the void.

He called it *making love*, but the things he did to her that night—everywhere but the bed—all of it was what Eugenia could only describe as fucking.

Primal. Passionate. Filthy.

Against the wall in the corner. Draped over the couch, her legs hooked on his arms. The floor as she tried to crawl to her pillow. In no part of his room did he not violate her.

In no encounter did she not give what she got.

Were it a game, were there a scoreboard… he cried out her name three times more than she cried out his.

She won.

And took her victory to a soft bed, held by a hard man, smiling as she dreamed of pizza and the medical wonders that once upon a time could be found on the internet.

# Chapter Nineteen

Fingers pumping between tingling labia already smeared in his spend, the captain's hooded gaze drank her in.

A hazel focus rested between her spread legs, upon her heaving breasts. At a woman who bit at her lip—but not in the teasing way she so loved to egg him on with. In the desperate way of a virgin out of her depth.

"Come one more time on my fingers and I'll stop. If you don't, I'll make love to you again." With a cruel smirk, he added, "From behind."

Which she had come to learn did not mean his standard ass-in-the-air Level 15 fuck. It meant he'd keep his hand on her clit, press her belly to the mattress, straddle her clenched thighs, and sexually torture her until she saw stars.

Legs shaking and impossibly turned on, she snarled, "For the love of God, you pervert. Put that *thing* away! You've already fucked me twice this morning."

Chuckling, he circled her clit, dragging the pad of his thumb *just so* to make her eyes roll back. "Unless you want three loads, I better feel you squeezing these fingers. Try to fake it and I'll drag you into the dark, dark world of anal."

Her hips stopped grinding, a red brow cocked. "Did you just refer to your semen as a load?"

"Three times it is then." Roguish, evil, and eating up her sunlight, he ordered, "Up you get!"

"No! Jesus, Aaron. I'll come. Just keep… doing what you're doing. Or, fuck, just let me blow you. You need to stop ejaculating in me."

Grin growing all the larger, he purred, "You don't have a choice, remember? Let's get a baby in there, shall we?"

"If I don't have a choice, why did you end your statement with a question?" Which really was a valid point, not that he'd let her argue further. Not when he might flip her over and manhandle his way back inside.

Which was precisely what he did.

Stretching slippery tissue, teasing the parts of her that stole her breath and made her liquid, penetration was extended.

Slow and thorough, he rode. Holding her hands, wrist to wrist, at the small of her back. Making her feel every last inch of him while he strummed her clit.

"You were made for this cock."

Which he could now fully fit inside her. A medical marvel, one might say.

Not that she could think straight or even answer when he did this to her.

"I love you." He said it so often, with such certainty.

And it set her off in a spin. Pussy fluttering, bucking back against him for more, she cried out and rode the edge of climax.

Right there, all she needed was one more piercing thrust.

As if he could feel her desperation around his glans, he teased at the gate, working her up by moving too slow with his cock and too fast with his fingers.

Pinned as she was, she could do nothing but arch and squirm.

No man should have a dick that thick, but her tormentor did. "This is how you tell me you love me, Eugenia. Tell me by coming for me. By taking what I have to give. I know, for now, you can't say it any other way."

Which wasn't fair, because she was spiraling out of control, wracked by a full-blown climax from little more than husky words and a sure thrust forward. Perfect penetration that hit everything inside her—that she was forced to feel thanks to the world's most wonderful position squeezing her around a relentless invasion.

She had no choice.

Felt his cock kick, heard his throaty groans, aware he unabashedly came undone. That he wanted her to have all of him. Knowing he wanted to be inside every part of her.

Which twisted her up in beautiful knots, each one unraveling as he said something sweet. Feeling his cock pump semen, the throb, the jump, the way he pinned her in place as he gave.

As she received, aching for more. Afraid of herself and the things he could entice.

"And I'll always love you, Eugenia." Full weight pressing her down, pinning her as he did each time he got his way, he prevented her from rushing to the bathroom to wash his seed away.

Panting, irritated, and thoroughly fucked, she snarled, "Don't think I don't realize what you're doing."

Draped over her back, sweaty and breathless, he asked, "Are you sore?"

A little. "Just say it. Get it over with…"

"You haven't tried to escape in a week."

"Raiding the kitchen is not an escape attempt. Besides, if you leave the door unlocked and then can't find me. Perhaps think it through before you come charging like a bull and rip of my panties."

Low warning was growled at her ear. "You're not allowed on Level 15 and you know it. Which is why I fucked you on the table when I found you."

Which had been seen by more people than Eugenia was ever going to think about. Hell, he had drawn a crowd. His palm over her mouth, her arguments trapped. And even with all the wide-eyed scampering women fleeing the room, she came… so fast she hadn't been prepared. And then he'd made her a sandwich.

Which she was forced to eat at that same table, while his cum leaked through her skirt and left a wet mark on the chair.

The sandwich had been good.

His angry glares had been better, though he was clearly baiting her.

Like he baited her with normal clothing. With Joan's offerings of strawberries that were not farmed in winter from hidden fields in the dead wood.

All of it leading to the one place he wanted her to accept.

A place that sent a shiver up her spine when it passed her lips on an unsettled whisper. "You're taking me to Level 9."

Though he was spent, he thrust again. As if she felt like bliss and he'd never get enough. "And locking you in for the day."

Enough compliments already. Heart sinking, she frowned. "Playing pretend for the last few weeks has been fun. What a shame real life always ruins things."

"Oh, honey." Turning her in his arms, Aaron pressed a kiss to her pouting mouth. "I know you're scared, and I'm swearing to you it's going to be okay."

He hadn't lied to her yet, but the gauge of what *was and wasn't* okay was a largely gray area.

"Don't think you can keep me there if I don't want to stay."

Stern, he kissed her hard. "And *you* don't think I won't come after you no matter where you might wander off to. You belong here with me."

***

He'd walked her to the entrance of Level 9, kissed her on the mouth as if dropping the little woman off at slavery camp was the normal way to start a day. Whistling to himself, he left her there. Where she could have turned tail and ran.

She was tempted to.

Very tempted.

Instead, Eugenia mustered up the courage to enter, ready to face what he'd built with her own eyes.

Joan was waiting on the other side. "You're late."

In more ways than one. Which, if the captain was keeping his calendar, he knew. "Let's get this over with."

That earned her a smirk. Like mother like son. "Well, aren't you just a ray of sunshine this afternoon."

That was her—nauseous ray of sunshine, Eugenia ready for her tour.

"As you can see, the promenade's interior balconies have been converted into hanging edible gardens, of a sort. All refuse is mulched on ship. Level 6, same place chickens are kept to turn the mulch and fertilize it. Solar panels on the roof, though when spring storms come, they will be removed and stored." Joan continued, clearly proud of all she displayed. "That's always a fun month of cold showers and dark."

Which deserved an epic eye roll. "You really have no idea what it's like out there, do you, Joan?"

Halting so fast her bob swung, Joan turned, raising a finger. "Listen, young lady, you're Mrs.

Kingston now. How many times do I have to tell you it's appropriate to call me Mother?"

"My last name is York."

"Oh God." As if the idea were truly appalling, Joan groaned. "Of course you'd be one of those women who insists on keeping their last name."

Chuckling, because she had missed the banter, the petty squabbles, the normalcy, Eugenia said, "Just because he forces me to wear a ring and tells everyone we're married doesn't make it so."

"I already told you the same thing I told him. There are no pastors on board!" Irritated and a bit flappish, Joan added, "Just… adapt… and pay attention."

It really was too much fun to wind Joan up. "You know I'm an atheist, right?"

Closing her eyes and drawing in a deep, shoulder-rising breath, Joan bit her tongue.

"Aaron is too." Smirk in full effect, Eugenia asked, "Has he ever told you that?"

Visibly grinding her teeth, Joan said, "It's a phase."

"*Mother*, he's forty-one. It's not a phase."

"The Kingstons are Baptists. Period."

Tossing red curls behind her shoulder, Eugenia countered, "I'm a York."

"You are a Kingston! Now, shut up and focus. Gretchen is in the early stages of labor, and I don't have all day to pamper your whims like he does. You're one of many on this ship, and all of them are counting on you to do your part." Annoyance went to full-blown motherly threat. "And don't you dare ruin her birth by being difficult. You'll smile with the rest of the women and deliver the baby."

Was that why she'd been manipulated into conceding today? "I don't know how to deliver babies! My interest was in pediatrics. I don't give a fuck about adults. I'm not a doctor."

"Men are not allowed in here, making you the only doctor they can count on. Unless you want to tell Gretchen she has to waddle down to the medical bay and deliver away from her family and friends. Considering how much she's been looking forward to a female doctor, it would be extremely selfish of you to let her down."

But Eugenia wasn't a doctor, not by a longshot. "It would be safer. I have no practical experience. And at no point in academia did I study obstetrics."

Softening, Joan put a hand on her daughter-in-law's shoulder. "I've delivered dozens of babies, found my calling after the war. And I'll teach you. The rest, Dr. Herbert will pass down while you intern with him from nine to five, Monday to Friday."

The perfect bribe to buy her attention and even keep her tied to the boat. "Was it your idea or his?"

Muttering under her breath, Joan lost her patience. "Don't ask questions you already know the answer to. I'm only supporting this, because it's practical and unlikely to cause a stir."

"You pimp women on Level 15. Don't get all self-righteous with me, Madame."

"Your anger issues are incredibly unrefined. Do you think I snapped at the First Lady when she threatened to have my family killed should my dear, departed George vote against the president's agenda? No. I smiled, and I carried my weight."

"Senator Kingston would have voted for the potato's war anyway."

"Just like you will catch Gretchen's baby anyway… and also why I found the First Lady's behavior to be ridiculous in the extreme." As if Miss America herself, Joan added, "Did you know that dead bitch claimed I had her horrible dog hit by a car? It was all over the tabloids."

It was Eugenia's turn to grind her teeth. "I like dogs."

"You wouldn't have liked that dog… snappy, biting rat that it was. Real dogs don't fit in purses."

The older woman's logic was always interesting. "Which justifies what you did?"

Bickering evaporated, Joan utterly compelling. “Just wait until someone threatens your children. There is no length you won’t go to keep them safe. And I mean that. There is nothing you won’t do for your baby.”

And Eugenia was two weeks late…

The honeymoon was over, the likelihood of implantation high. Especially considering how many times she’d let him fuck her.

How many times they’d *made love*.

Even worse, Eugenia was *in love*.

Lord, she was going to be sick.

As if the older woman could read the terror in Eugenia’s eyes, she softened. “It’s too early to know for certain, but if it doesn’t happen this month, it *will* happen soon. Everyone is nervous with their first. What you feel right now is normal.”

“The circumstances are *not* normal.” Had her lip just shaken? She was never going to live it down.

Hooking Eugenia's arm, Joan passed down wisdom the way a mother had to a daughter since the dawn of humankind. "The new normal then. A healthy baby, born here. A child who will thrive in all this."

And *all this* was grand indeed, now that Eugenia was standing in the midst of it. A palace hidden at the center of the ship. The entirety carved into homes for families bursting with wide-eyed and happy children. Where women chatted, laughed, and breastfed their babies. Where orphans found mothers eager to hold them.

Where those who refused to submit to their duty had been moved somewhere on ship no soul would confess to the captain's wife.

Chilling, grotesque, and something Joan seemed all the happier for when she mentioned so bleak a topic in passing during the tour.

Yet, Brooke was there, wandering through the vegetation—slowly fighting her way out of shock. Surrounded by sisters who understood, who would be there for her. Who didn't mind when she wet herself or when she tore at her hair or clothes.

Who knew what to say, and the exact tone to say it in.

Because Eugenia was the outsider on Level 9.

The women watching made that clear. This was *their* home, and they would trample her into dust if she tried to take it from them.

And that was no light threat. One of those mothers alone was far more intimidating than any of the men Eugenia had encountered on the ship. All of them with families to protect, all of them willing to take up a weapon to keep what they had worked hard to build.

And the men had no idea.

Though as Eugenia was introduced to them one by one, she wondered if Aaron suspected. If that was the real reason he had not put her here after he pulled her from the lake.

Because she would not have needed him to bicker with. Not when there were sharp minds aplenty on Level 9. Because she might have found comfort in the arms of other women and submitted so she too could have a baby at her breast and community to enjoy.

Not that the captain had not been trying in earnest to see that potential outcome take place.

How one woman was supposed to take care of that oversized penis for the rest of her life, Eugenia didn't know.

Next thing she knew, she'd be doing morning yoga with the rest of the women. Barf.

"Did you hear what I said about drainage?"

Not really. "Yes, yes. Plant matter builds up and has to be routinely removed or the whole drainage system backs up."

Nodding approval, Joan continued her tour. And Eugenia followed.

Three hours later, they were called to join a woman loudly groaning through the pains of labor. One who had already delivered three babies—hyper fertile, as it were.

And happy.

Gretchen was happy to see a squalling infant placed on her breast, to hold her fourth child as it made its first cries.

Even though no father was there, and even though not one of her children resembled the next.

Looking down at the amniotic fluid, the vernix, the blood on her ungloved hands, having been the first to *catch* a newborn human, Eugenia felt her eyes burn.

And then she looked to Joan. Joan, who had walked her through each step in the surprisingly quick final moments of labor. And she meant every word. "Thank you."

The older woman smiled, saying, "You're not done yet. Gretchen still needs to deliver the placenta."

Which was a fascinating organ to inspect in real life. Until it was taken away to be steamed and dehydrated. To be eaten by the mother with her daily meals. Full of hormones that would help her body recover from the strain.

Which was sound science, Eugenia supposed.

# Chapter Twenty

"Are you hungry? Dinner is waiting."

Hungry? Always. Exhilarated? Absolutely.

No guard or watchful eye had escorted her from Level 9 to the captain's rooms. Not anymore.

Sitting was… a challenge, now that a tiny foot had taken residence against her right ribs. Getting up, belly larger by the day, was almost impossible. Not that it stopped her from plopping down on the couch with a tired sigh.

Head lolling against the cushion, Eugenia shut her eyes. "I'm just going to take a nap real quick."

Lips came to her forehead. "You've never looked more beautiful."

"Shut up, Aaron." She felt like a whale. A striped whale who clearly had not received the no-stretch-mark gene.

He put a plate on her belly. One that balanced just fine. “Eat. You’ll feel better.”

Roast pumpkin with onions and fish. Everything she craved since waking that morning and telling him how badly she needed it. Gloriously delicious as she scarfed it down like an animal. And then she did feel better. Like a new woman even. One even willing to talk to the handsome man taking off her shoe.

“I set a broken leg today. Compound fracture. A real mess.” Smiling, she met his eyes. “You should have seen it.”

Laughing, he removed her other shoe. “I’ll let the men know you’re looking forward to their suffering.”

“Ugh, I need to pee again.” Said with such desolation for her imminent loss of comfort on the couch.

“Up you go.” Plate set aside, he heaved his extremely pregnant wife to standing.

And stole a kiss before she might escape. One that rode her moods and altered their course until she was relaxed against him with a small smile on her mouth.

Lashes parting, she found his gaze as warm as it always was, and then her smile became a frown. "You know, they hate that I'm forced to leave Level 9 and come here every night. Those women, they don't know what you're really like. They only know what you did to them."

Too many of the women on Level 9 had been fucked too hard by an indifferent, evil man. Some of them had once thought themselves in love, until they realized what he'd put them through on Level 15. Others had never seen him save the first time they stepped onto the boat. How he'd coldly outlined what their lives would be before throwing them into isolation for a month to adjust.

Not that all those new women made it to Level 9 anymore. Those who truly refused went… somewhere else, hidden from Eugenia to be bred.

Babies were delivered upstairs in need of a breast, fresh from the womb and squalling.

Eugenia had almost killed him the first time, slicing Captain so badly with his dinner knife Dr. Herbert had been called to stitch him when she refused.

On his knees, weeping when she swore she'd never look at him again, he pleaded that the mother promised to kill the baby. Swearing that she had murdered the one before—that the little boy wasn't safe with her. That all the complicated cases were well fed and as clean as the women would allow themselves to be. *That he didn't have a choice.*

Eugenia still didn't speak to him for a week.

Staying with Brooke, who was far more pregnant and far more coherent when Eugenia came sobbing to her door.

Who told her to pull her head out of her ass.

Because she had seen the captain and his favorite captive. Because, out of all the women on Level 9, Brooke knew how much they loved one another and never told a soul. “The world out there is fire and pain. Some bring the pain back here where it’s safe. The captain can’t let it spread.”

Eugenia, in the most fucked-up way, had the dream all of them had yearned for.

Yet her voice still had to be heard. “He has women on the boat he forces to reproduce… and then he takes away their children.”

Scar tissue distorting her smile, Brooke offered a lopsided and honest grin. “And good for those women for refusing. And good for him for saving a life.”

“It’s rape.” The ugliest of words.

“It is.” A thing Brooke knew well, a word that set her eyelid twitching. “But I know it’s not like… what happened to me.”

“Brooke.” Eugenia took her friend’s hand, tears on her cheek. “It’s exactly like what happened to you.”

Brushing back her friend’s curls, Brooke whispered, “Yet you love him anyway.”

And Eugenia cried all the harder.

Because she did. She loved him so much that sometimes it hurt to breathe.

While self-sequestered on Level 9, she held that new baby, feeling her own quicken inside. Watched the women fawn over him, how they gladly shared the duty of breastfeeding him. Absorbed that the child was one of theirs and would be loved.

Slept all day, all night, for a week. Woke up to find a new tube of cherry Chapstick had been curled into her fingers while she dreamed.

And went home after the sun went down to find a wretched man badly in need of a shower and a shave.

"They've named him Noah." Setting down her candle, she added, "I never want to know who fathered him, because if he comes to my clinic, I'll kill him."

Eyes wet, the captain agreed. "Fair enough."

"I mean it. Hide it from me until the day I die."

Aaron nodded.

"How are the stitches healing?" There had to be at least twenty across his chest the way she'd sliced him.

It was as if he hadn't heard her, as if he might not be able to draw another breath unless he said, "I love you."

"I know you do." Which broke her heart a little bit more. He loved her so deeply Eugenia sometimes drowned in it.

Nodding at the unspoken ugliness between them, he asked, "Are you hungry?"

"Always."

They ate by candlelight.

Months passed, their baby grew.

Another motherless newborn was passed to Level 9.

Eugenia felt doubt. She felt fear.

They didn't speak of it. And, no matter how hard she searched, she could not find where those unwilling women were kept on the boat.

Aaron lavished her with attention, with affection, with bouts of sex that scratched an endless itch pregnancy had inspired.

He tolerated her moods, her sulks. Celebrated her joys.

The pair of them honored a silent agreement that some part of her would always hate him, and the greater part of him would swallow that hate and turn it into love.

Not that he deserved her. She definitely didn't deserve him. Yet there they were, their baby on the horizon. Her bladder full, his smile gentle.

"Honey'," he said, cupping her cheek. "It doesn't matter what the women think. When we're in here, what's out there isn't privy to our secrets."

With a sigh, she looked down at the belly between them. At a baby who was running out of space and due to be born.

"Which is why I deserve you." She deserved the burden of the other women's concern and question of her judgment. Because she would never tell them she'd stolen the one thing not one of them would have.

"You had a long day and you're tired." Easing her toward the restroom, he ordered, "Use the toilet. I'll have a surprise waiting."

Grumbling, she obeyed. "The only thing surprising about your dick these days is that a man your age can still keep it up."

Ignoring her sass, she was left in silence to pee. And came back to the room to find him holding up her coat.

Which, in all fairness, was surprising. "I'm not feeling up to a stroll about the deck." Not when she'd hear the party on Level 15.

His smile grew, hazel gaze twinkling. "How about a moonlit boat ride on the lake?"

Expression excited, she blurted, "I want to walk on the shore."

Wild dogs howled in the night.

With nothing but adoration shining from his eyes, he refused, “No.”

**Thank you for reading Swallow it Down! Ready for more? Dystopian, dark, delicious, turn the page for a full chapter excerpt of BRANDED now!**

**Craving more? Omegaverse Dark Romance at its most gut-wrenching! Jealous, possessive, and willing to commit any sin to steal his mate, Shepherd is the antihero book boyfriend you've been waiting for.**

•Born to be Bound — Violent, calculating, and incapable of remorse, Shepherd demands his new mate's adoration. Her attention. Her body.

•Born to be Broken — He doesn't know how to love his captive Omega. But Shepherd is determined to learn.

•Reborn — the nature of their pair-bond has consumed Claire to the point that she has difficulty differentiating where her feelings begin and Shepherd's machinations end.

•Stolen —He took her with violence while none intervened. He broke her, swearing he'd put her back together.

**The Wren's Song Series is a dark, sinister Omegaverse Reverse Harem tale for those with twisted tastes and a love for complete power exchange.**

•Branded Captive — Wren can't sing like a bird. She can't speak at all. The Alpha kingpin and his pack didn't buy the Omega to hear it talk.

•Silent Captive — Wren is caught in the clutches of three dangerous Alphas, each with their own selfish designs.

•Broken Captive — Caspian has marked her, Toby has claimed her, and Kieran is unwillingly caught in her spell.

•Ravaged Captive — Drenched in wealth and power, Caspian holds my city by the throat. No man or woman denies him, not even me.

**Carnal, filthy, and unbelievably satisfying. My bestselling Omegaverse Dark Romance awaits those daring enough to take a taste.**

•The Golden Line — They call me brutal. They call me unrepentant. They call me possessive. I am all these things and much, much worse.

**Like your men in doting, affectionate, and utterly possessive? Read my Reverse Harem Dark Romance. The Irdesi Empire Series is smoldering page-turner sure to satisfy.**

•Sigil — He will have her. Even if he must crush empires. Even if he must harm her for her own good. Even if he must share her with his brothers. Sigil will be his.

•Sovereign — Sovereign tends his reluctant consort. His many Brothers lavish her with attention, each exercising their own brand of seduction to woo their species' only female.

**If your tastes run to brooding alpha males, my hit dark romance, this Regency Dark Romance will scratch your itch.**

•Dark Side of the Sun — Greedy, cunning, cruel, Gregory claims to love her, offers to kill for her… but lies come easily to his tongue.

**Obsession and the most twisted "love" fill this smoldering page-turner. Beware, the dark horror ahead.**

•Catacombs — The vampire king has found his queen, locking her away for his own sick pleasures.

**Taboo horror that will worm its way into your darker thoughts and keep you up all night? Whatever you do, don't follow the white rabbit!**

•The White Queen — The devil owes the Hatter a favor… and he knows just what he wants for his prize.

•Immaculate — But my knees have been sullied in worship to a vacant altar. Everything I was taught is a lie. There is no God here.

**Love good, old fashioned desire? Take a turn with this prohibition era romance.**

•A Taste of Shine — Something isn't right about the new girl in town. Charlotte Elliot swears, she drinks, and she's trying too damn hard to fit in with the simple folk.

•A Shot in the Dark — Matthew is determined to find his run-away sweetheart. And then he's going to marry her.

**Now, please enjoy an extended excerpt of Branded**

# BRANDED

*Wren's Song, Book One*

## Chapter 1

"Accept my seed, Omega."

The breath wafting over her cheek was rancid, but it was the last thing Wren might take stock of when that *thing* was cracking her pelvis in half. She had done as she'd been instructed. Remained docile when the man had yanked her legs embarrassingly wide over his thighs. She had even ignored the thick thatch of coarse salt and pepper hair on his chest scratching her back when he hoisted her up.

He'd growled as her mother told her he would, and torn through her barrier with one impatient yank of her hips. Unable to scream, Wren had only arched her spine, head thrown back on his shoulder. The Alpha, either oblivious or uncaring for her comfort, grasped her hips, bobbing her up and down his veined cock three times. With the fourth rude shunt, he'd clawed at her softer places and driven her down until her cheeks slapped against his lap. Immediately something ballooned inside aching guts. It pressed her bladder to the point Wren was certain she'd dribbled more than a little piss on her new mate, continuing to expand until squished bowels, organs, and jangled nerves all screamed for relief.

"Damn you, Omega. Take my seed!"

Take what where? She didn't understand what she was supposed to do now.

At her back, the stranger panted, shifting beneath her as if he too were extremely uncomfortable. When she failed to perform, his irritation quickly translated into anger. The stink invaded Wren's nostrils, it made her skin buzz.

Angry Alphas killed.

Angry Alphas must always be appeased.

Staring forward across the dimly lit, yet finely appointed space, Wren inhaled and exhaled on a count of three. There was nothing to be done about the stinging stretch where her legs were hooked over the man's spread thighs. He had not offered to take her to a bed or even asked to see her build a nest. No, the couch in his fine house's receiving room had suited his purpose well enough.

Examine and test the stock.

Fuck the virgin with her father on the other side of the cracked door.

The man who'd brought his Omega daughter to sell listening to this. To the Alpha's strained breaths, to his grunts and wheezing.

Her father was listening to her failure.

Wren forced herself to look down. She had not seen the Alpha's cock before he'd shunted it unexpectedly into her, or even had a good look at the male. Her eyes had been downcast when they arrived, lest her father strike her for insolence. She had disrobed for inspection. She had moved as commanded and not resisted when the Alpha yanked her to the nearest seat.

And her father had exited the room to listen so he might claim full payment for what transpired.

Payment for... *this*. Wren stared where only the root of an Alpha cock was visible stretching her labia beyond imagining. There was a little blood, far less than she'd anticipated considering the burn. The red spread with their fluids, matting the hair that peppered his swollen ball sack.

The knot in her belly gave an angry pulse, expanding again in a bid to ruin her completely. Gnashing his teeth, the Alpha almost whined against her neck, his balls thundering in twitching pulses. They too expanded, the skin under all that coarse hair growing shiny and white from the stretch.

"Fucking Omega…" A meaty hand left her hip, landing on her belly as if that might force her even further down his meat. But there was nowhere else to go. She was tied to him by that pulsating knot spreading agony in her guts. From the way he fought to speak, how his breath hitched in a whine with each breath, the Alpha was in as much pain as she. "You have one purpose. Milk my fucking cock!"

If that knot kept banging against her pubic bone, she was going to be sick all over his rug. Stalled, unsure what it was he wanted from her, Wren thought the wisest course was to remain still and wait.

It was the wrong choice.

"Your freak daughter is failing to comply!" The snarled shout was directed to the cracked door.

The meek response was never the tone Wren's father took with her. "Have you… umm… stimulated her, sir?"

Wren's new owner turned his head, yelling so sharply the girl flinched. "Of course I have! She belligerently refuses to bring me to orgasm. My fucking knot is full. Gah—" Slick with sweat, the Alpha squeezed her tighter, caught in a waving cramp of his own. "I'll have your goddamn head for this, Carson!"

"Wren, honey." Through the cracked door, her father sing-songed, "Relax and take his seed. Show this illustrious Alpha you wish to serve as his mate."

She wanted to sign that I didn't understand, to reach out for the man who'd brought her there to sell her. But he could not see.

Her potential mate roared, "SEND IN HELENA!"

Another door in the chilly room opened, a woman in a vivid robe rushing forward. "How can I serve you, my Alpha?"

"Bend over the desk and wait for me!"

Wren watched the woman quickly strip, viewing another naked female body for the first time in her life. With no preamble, the pretty brunette bent at the waist, the globes of her ass presented, her cheek to the wood.

Beta female parts were on display.

Cruel fingers reached for Wren's stretched labia, the Alpha yanking at the sensitive flesh as he grunted and threw her forward with his weight. His ballooning testicles doubled in size, the man groaning with the worst sort of agony.

His pain was nothing to hers. The knot that was meant to tie them together in life was deformed by his tricks until it could be pulled free of her body. Wren was dumped on the floor, hand pressed between her trembling legs as she wailed.

From the corner of her eye, she watched the Alpha scythe his cock into the waiting female, wrecking her with the madness of his need to release. Unlike Wren, the Beta gave him immediate relief, the Alpha's cry earsplitting.

Bowed over, curled in on herself, Wren shut her eyes to it all.

When her father was called forward, even then she refused to rise to meet his gaze. Naked and shamed on the floor of a stranger's house, she sniffed, wishing she couldn't hear the terrible things that were said about her.

"Was she not trained?"

"My wife took great pains to explain what would be expected, sir. You have my humblest apologies that she failed, but if you are not going to take her as your new mate, you still owe for the tearing of her hymen. She will be harder to sell unintact."

Of course her father would try to weasel credits from this man…

The Alpha gave an incredulous laugh. "Your mute albino freak might be pretty to look at, but she is the worst fuck imaginable. If you think I'd expose that cunt to another Alpha in this city, you're wrong."

"You owe me one-thousand credits for her virginity!" Her father never once came to her defense, never offered her comfort, he only tried to squeeze what he could from a far richer man. "The contract was clear. No matter the outcome of the first mating, a fee will be paid!"

The sound of ice hitting the side of crystal, the pour of liquor. Far calmer, the Alpha took a long sip. "The contract," a smile in his voice, the Alpha purred, "is null and void if the merchandise is defective. You get nothing, Carson. She will be tagged and dumped in the Warrens and you will leave here grateful to be breathing."

No! Ignoring sore muscles and the screaming pain between her legs, Wren scampered to her father and wrapped her arm around his leg. Signing frantically, she begged him for mercy.

He looked down at his pale, violet-eyed child, deadpan as he said, "I should have had you euthanized at birth."

**Read BRANDED now!**

# Addison Cain

USA TODAY bestselling author and Amazon Top 25 bestselling author, Addison Cain is best known for her dark romances, smoldering Omegaverse, and twisted alien worlds. Her antiheroes are not always redeemable, her lead females stand fierce, and nothing is ever as it seems.

Deep and sometimes heart wrenching, her books are not for the faint of heart. But they are just right for those who enjoy unapologetic bad boys, aggressive alphas, and a hint of violence in a kiss.

Visit her website:

addisoncain.com

*Don't miss these exciting titles by Addison Cain!*

Swallow it Down

Strangeways

The Golden Line

**The Alpha's Claim Series:**
Born to be Bound

Born To Be Broken
Reborn
Stolen
Corrupted

**Wren's Song Series:**
Branded
Silenced

**The Irdesi Empire Series:**
Sigil
Sovereign
Que: Book Three (coming soon)

**Cradle of Darkness Series:**
Catacombs
Cathedral
The Relic

**A Trick of the Light Duet:**
A Taste of Shine
A Shot in the Dark

**Historical Romance:**
Dark Side of the Sun

**Horror:**
The White Queen
Immaculate

CPSIA information can be obtained
at www.ICGtesting.com
Printed in the USA
LVHW110016140822
725894LV00019B/145